T0147024

Titles by ▲

Osagyefo
The Great Betrayal

A Historical Novel

Linus T. Asong

Langaa Research & Publishing CIG
Mankon, Bamenda

Publisher:
Langaa RPCIG
Langaa Research & Publishing Common Initiative Group
P.O. Box 902 Mankon
Bamenda
North West Region
Cameroon
Langaagrp@gmail.com
www.langaa-rpcig.net

Distributed outside N. America by African Books
Collective
orders@africanbookscollective.com
www.africanbookscollective.com

Distributed in N. America by Michigan State
University Press
msupress@msu.edu
www.msupress.msu.edu

ISBN: 9956-616-38-9

DISCLAIMER

Contents

Acknowledgement

In coming up with this highly dramatic and fictionalized version of Kwame Nkrumah's very rich life, I owe a huge debt of gratitude to:

1. June Milne whose well documented book *KWAME NKRUMAH: A BIOGRAPHY* (PANAF BOOKS, 1999, 75 Weston Street, London, SE1 3RS), I milked for anything that I found necessary for my purpose.

2. T. Peter Omari from whose book *KWAME NKRUMAH: THE ANATOMY OF AN AFRICAN DICTATORSHIP* (Moxon Paperbacks, Accra, 1970) I borrowed much of the material that constituted the dialogue sections.

3. *NEW AFRICAN* magazine, especially Numbers 460 of March 2007, from which I gleaned information on the subject of betrayals along with the story of Nkrumah's visit to Lincoln and the invitation he made to Africans of the Diaspora.

4. *WEST AFRICA*, Number 4139 of 3-9 March 1997, from which I first got the story of Yaasei, Kotoka's so-called teacher in my book.

5. *BBC FOCUS ON AFRICA* MAGAZINE of January – March 2007, from which I got more reliable information surrounding Nkrumah's marriage to Fathia Rizk, from Nkrumah's son himself, Gamel.

6. John Stockwell's book, *IN SEARCH OF ENEMIES* (London, 1978), from which I got details and confirmation on the CIA's direct involvement in the overthrow of Nkrumah.

7. Dr. George Atem with whom I had many discussions during our days at Cape Coast made me develop an interest in Kwame Nkrumah's life and writings during our University of Cape Coast days, and from whose extremely rich library on Nkrumah I borrowed books to help me realise my goal in this work.

8. Other works which provided me with insights I cannot directly pinpoint, but which I found invaluable in building up my case for and against Nkrumah. These include: Stephen Dzirasa's *THE POLITICAL THOUGHTS OF DR. KWAME NKRUMAH* (Accra, Guinea Press, 1962); Kwesi Armah's *AFRICA'S GOLDEN ROAD* (London, Heinemann, 1965); F. M. Bouret's *GHANA: THE ROAD TO INDEPENDENCE* (OUP, 1960); Kwame Nkrumah's *DARK DAYS IN GHANA* (PANAF, 1968), *HANDBOOK OF REVOLUNIONARY WARFARE* (PANAF, 1968); *AFRICA MUST UNITE* (PANAF, 1963); *CONSCIENCISM*, Kwame Nkrumah's

The struggle continues

Foreword

This book is first and foremost a novel, implying that it is basically a work of fiction. Therefore, the characters, the episodes and the issues at stake may not be historically realistic. But, even more than that, *Osagyefo: The Great Betrayal* is a historical novel; therefore, although the characters and the situations, and dialogue may be products of the imagination, at the heart of the novel is a character and a situation that did, in fact, take place. The inspiration to write such a novel stemmed from the mass of material I encountered some years ago while working on (*Nde Ntumazah: A Conversational Autobiography*). This is the story of another enigmatic and elusive freedom fighter as well as Kwame Nkrumah's personal friend.

I discovered that the period between 1950 and 1965 was extremely rich and challenging, and that the political leaders of the time were all, without exception, activists of larger than life characters and whose lives sounded more strange than fiction. The unfortunate thing about African political leaders these days is that they do not make interesting subjects for fiction: while in office they are sacrosanct even in their endless vices; and when out of office they become so anathema that no writer of talent would spend useful time on them.

Let us say that I got carried away by the fascinating nature of their adventures or misadventures to the extent that I treated some of them with less respect than they deserved. If that is the case anywhere in this book, I can only ask for forgiveness from those whose idols I have treated with levity. As for the characters that exist nowhere in history like Ebny Whitestone, I have no apologies to offer to anybody. My creative mind tells me that if a character ever existed like that, and if it is true that the CIA had its hand in the overthrow of Nkrumah, then he must have behaved precisely or nearly as precisely as I have conceived him to achieve the goal.

L. T. Asong

Chapter One

Ebny Whitestone was what is termed in smokers' jargon "a chain smoker." He smoked at least five packets of twenty sticks of cigarettes each, each day, and in between he smoked cigars in rapid succession as well. When he was as disturbed as or as anxious about something as he was that evening, he pumped cigar and cigarette fumes into his lungs in a non-stop connection. He had already discarded three cigarette would-be stubs or leftovers in the large clay ashtray without running half the length of each stick, and was now on his second cigar. With the cigar clenched between his chiselled, tobacco-stained teeth, he was pacing up and down in his secretariat - a large vestibule that looked more or less a sitting room in a rich merchant's palace.

He was a big man in all senses of the word, and must have bigger once before, because his large jacket hung loosely by a pair of suspenders, over his equally loose waistline of the blue pair of velvet jeans he wore. He stood close to two metres in height and had the muscles of a professional wrestler or heavy weight boxer. To be sure, many people meeting him for the first time thought he was in the wrong profession, and that instead of sitting behind a mahogany desk hauling objects not heavier than a pencil he would have been in the *wrestlemania* ring hauling other wrestlers over the ropes, or lifting weights at the Olympics or sparing with Mohamed Ali or George Foreman.

In point of fact, the observers were never far from the truth because Ebny Whitestone's muscles had not been entirely wasted. He had been a basketball player and featured in a few matches for the Los Angeles Lakers in the early

1

sixties before a knee injury sent him into early retirement. He was over fifty, or even sixty. His hair was already greying at the temples, and his fairly full face just missed being fleshy. He wore heavy, steel-rimmed spectacles which kept rolling down and narrowing his nostrils somewhat, compelling him every now and then to use his right forefinger to push them back into place. Although on record he passed for an African-American, he was so light that with just a little bit of relaxing on his thickly cropped and spongy hair you would consider him a white man who has had a good tan. This look was accentuated by the fact that due to constant use over the years, the heavy spectacles had almost closed his otherwise flat nostrils, giving them a pointed European shape.

With a heavy right hand he pulled the left sleeve of his coffee-brown shirt slightly upward and glanced at his golden wristwatch. It was already 8 pm, and he was supposed to have met his men since 7.30.

"Shert mein!" he cursed. "African time!" he mumbled angrily at the African's carefree attitude towards punctuality of time. He would never get used to that, he thought. In this particular venture, this extremely delicate mission, there was no room for failure. His entire government would be discredited. If the people did not turn up it meant only one thing: betrayal. They must have betrayed him to Kwame Nkrumah whom, he knew from experience, was not above calling a press conference just to ridicule his government, ordering his arrest or doing something as absurd as that. After all, he had already pulled Ghana out of the Commonwealth and could just as well sever relations with the U.S. It would have been better not to raise the issue at all and let Nkrumah go on with his nefarious activities. It would be worse than letting Nkrumah do as he pleased.

He was saved further ruminations and anxiety when he heard a strange rattling noise. He went out to the balcony and peered through the darkness. Yes, there was a vehicle very near his residence. He walked back to his office in a hurry. If the people came and found him on the balcony they might think that he was worried about their delay. Although that was a fact, he did not want to create that impression. He has to make it look like he personally had nothing to gain from the exercise. He glanced at his watch, it was now twenty minutes after the hour of eight. On second thought, when the car, an old Vox Wagon rattled to a halt outside his gate he changed his mind. It was important for the men to keep their disguises on until they got into his office upstairs.

He climbed down the stairs with quick athletic steps, too fast for a man of that bulk and even that age. He arrived at the car just in time to warn the lone visitor who wore a turban in the typical northern style – wrapped several times round his head and round his chin, a false beard and photo chronic sunglasses.

"You are alone?" he asked the visitor, looking into the back seat of the car which was empty.

"Am alone," the visitor replied. "My man not yet here?"

"Not yet."

"He will soon be here."

"Drive in and park there," he pointed to a corner inside the fence. The man did and then climbed down. The two men walked back up, saying nothing to each other, Ebny Whitestone glancing constantly over his shoulder just in case any intruder was observing them. They passed through the vast secretariat which the visitor was seeing for the first time. There were about six electric typewriters, each covered with a thick cloth to protect it against dust. Each of them stood in the centre of a large well polished, wooden table with three drawers on either side of a high revolving chair, most likely for the secretaries. On both sides of the typewriters were IN and OUT trays containing envelopes and files, some open and others still sealed. There was a low, long, central table surrounded by smaller armchairs and on which lay several newspapers and magazines, ashtrays and three flower vases. A little to the right of the table stood an American flag on a small pole of about half a metre.

The two men passed through the secretariat towards a large panelled door to the extreme right corner of the wall that bore it. Above the panelled door hung in a fancifully decorated silver frame the picture of President Lyndon B. Johnson, President of America. Not so long ago, it was that of President John F. Kennedy that hung there. But it was pulled down immediately after his assassination by Lee Oswald. Ebny Whitestone simply turned the door knob to the right and pushed and went in.

"Come on in and make yourself comfortable," he told his guest.

The stranger hesitated for only a brief second and then began to undo his disguise. The air in the office was fresh and this was hardly surprising because the air conditioning system was perfect.

"Make yourself comfortable," Ebny Whitestone told the visitor again, trying to generate in him a self-control he did not possess himself at that particular moment. "And welcome."

"Thank you," the stranger replied with almost exaggerated meekness, a point which Whitestone took mental note of. The stranger was Colonel Emmanuel Kotoka, Commander of the Second Infantry Group of the Ghanaian army. The Ambassador showed him a seat and then went on to ask:

"Something to drink? Some coffee? Tea? Some juice, beer, brandy, whisky? Anything you would like." He was talking and pulling a small table on wheels bearing a globe showing the five continents. He clutched the North pole with his thumb, forefinger and index finger and pulled it, disclosing its contents of assorted drinks.

4

Colonel Kotoka looked at it with great admiration, glanced at his watch but refused to take anything. Apparently he was waiting for his colleague, the second person being expected. It was his own turn now to be worried. If his colleague failed to turn up, there could be only one explanation: betrayal. In that case he would take away his own life rather than face the humiliation of being paraded through the streets of Accra as a traitor. He had come ready, his revolver ready for any eventuality. As he looked uneasily round the room, the American Ambassador who was also still worried, reassured him:

"Feel completely free and secure in here. I am completely alone. I sent my entire household away. I wanted us to talk in absolute secrecy. I will receive no intruders, no visitors. As soon as your colleague comes I will shut the gate myself and lock it."

"O.K," Colonel Kotoka said, breathing nervously. The two of them really needed to be there present, he thought again. But he fought to conceal his worry. There would be no room for excuses. One man absent was just as bad or worse than the two of them staying away.

On the low, wooden table between them stood the picture of some black athlete, framed in gold. Kotoka who had himself been an athlete in his secondary school days bent towards it with some concealed curiosity.

"That's you?" he asked to relieve himself of the tension that was building up.

"No. Jesse Owens. The great Jesse Owens," the man said and then asked: "You should know him."

Kotoka looked closely but confessed: "I am not sure."

"Jesse Owens was that famous black man, the first ever, who won four gold medals at the Berlin Olympics in 1936. Adolf Hitler couldn't stand that, seeing that a coloured man had beaten his best German athletes to that top spot."

Kotoka nodded although he had never heard of that.

"That is my maternal uncle," Ebny Whitestone said proudly. "We are from the direct line of great athletes...."

He would have said more, but mercifully, there was a distant noise which grew louder and louder as it approached the residence of the Ambassador. He went to the window and pulled the curtain to one side and looked out but could not see much. He went to the secretariat and looked out. A taxi had halted in front of his gate. He heaved a sigh of relief and ran down with the same nimble steps just in time to warn the strange to keep on the disguise until they had entered his office. He showed the second stranger where to park, far away from his colleague. The two men then went up, through the secretariat and into his office.

"Akwa-abaa!" Colonel Kotoka greeted his compatriot.

"Yohhh," the man responded.

Ebny Whitestone went to the door into the secretariat and shut it and keyed it. He entered his office, shut the door too and keyed it and then watched the second visitor take off his disguise. The second stranger was Major A.A. Afrifa of the Second Brigade of the Ghanaian army. He had come wearing a large over coat that covered even his shoes, with a raised collar over a thick cotton muffler. On his head was an oversized cowboy hat complete with a string running round his chin. He was also wearing a pair of dark glasses so that it was impossible for a casual observer to recognise him. And, having a natural gift for mimicry, he completely disguised his voice too.

"You are very smart guys, you two," the Ambassador said, referring to the various forms of disguise they had put on. "Who would know you were the ones?"

"We really thought about it well," Kotoka said, congratulating themselves.

. The Ambassador pulled open the north pole of the cellar and proposed drinks and coffee or tea. The mood had suddenly become lighter, and understandably so.

6

"A small whisky won't kill me," Afrifa said

"Me too, some whisky," Kotoka said. "How can I be drinking coffee at this time?"

The Ambassador laughed and Kotoka grinned and turned to Afrifa and told him that the Ambassador was laughing because he had proposed a drink earlier and he had turned it down. The Ambassador took his seat behind his large oak desk, holding a newspaper which he was pretending to read. But he was actually studying the two men and working out in his mind how he would win them over. Looking above his glasses and over the newspaper he fixed his gaze on them both. They were exactly what he expected to find: dry, serious and without any trace of humour whatsoever about them. Under their disguise both soldiers were wearing their army uniforms, complete with their epaulets.

They both wore dark green trousers with heavy leather belts girding the waist over the shirts. Afrifa seemed shorter than Kotoka by a head and was probably younger, rather thin of face, he was well built, with broad shoulders, and his thinness of face with the skin drawn tightly over his prominent cheekbones, gave him a hardened, energetic look. Like most Africans, he had a large broad nose and a wide mouth and a sharp chin. One thing struck Ebny Whitestone about him: the high forehead and below it the deeply set small eyes which looked piercingly at any observer.

Kotoka was almost of the same mould, though slightly taller. He was of medium height, sprouted a beard and a thin moustache above slightly sarcastic set of strong, sharply curved lips. His eyes looked sullenly calm but one easily saw that this was a man used to giving orders and who did not entertain arguments. To the expression of military or official hardness on his face, which is peculiar to soldiers of high rank in Africa, was also added that aura of power. This suited Ebny Whitestone's purpose very well. But one more thing impressed him about them which his security reports had taken time to establish: they looked naïve and wanting in self confidence, and not so knowledgeable about many things, a failing he must exploit to its fullest.

Chapter Two

When he was sure that he had studied them enough and that they must have taken a good sip of the whisky, he kept the newspaper aside, walked round the massive desk and came to sit backing the door, facing the two men such that Kotoka was to his right and Afrifa to his left.

"And how did your seminar go?" he asked them both.

"It is still on," Kotoka replied. "It is good, so far so good," he added and then sat up and folded his hands over his chest, expecting to hear from the Ambassador. Of course he knew that the man had not invited them to find out about the seminar. Ebny Whitestone knew that too and so did not even pretend about it.

"Let me go straight to the point, gentlemen," he said, putting aside his cigar for a while. "I called you here so that you and I should take stock of the economic and political situation in Ghana."

Kotoka smiled. Taking stock of the political situation in Ghana? What did they as soldiers know to the extent of taking stock? As if reading his thoughts exactly, the Ambassador said:

"I know that as soldiers you may not have much to say about that, but even the very little that you know, you may be surprised to find how important it is to our discussion this evening."

The two officers exchanged meaningful glances while nodding dubiously at the same time.

"Let me be even more explicit, if somebody came from say, South Africa now, and asked you about Ghana what would you say?"

"Asking about Ghana as from what time, Mr. Ambassador?" Kotoka asked a bit unclear as the question.

"Good question. Let's say since independence," the Ambassador put in. Because of the squinted nature of his eyes, neither Kotoka nor Afrifa knew exactly who he was looking at. In the end Afrifa volunteered an attempt:

"I would say we have tried to do many things, build schools, open roads like the motorway, built dams, eh my man?" he turned to his colleague.

"Yes, it is so," Kotoka concurred. "he head of state has been inviting different heads of state to come here for conferences. Many many things."

The Ambassador was nodding. He then reached for his cigar, shook off the ash into the tray, pulled at it for a moment and then said:

"That is well said. That sounds like all is very well with Ghana. Everything just going like clockwork, according to plan. No problems whatsoever…"

"Oh no, no, no, Mr. Ambassador. That's not what I mean. We have our problems, quite all right, just like all other countries do, but we are also trying to achieve many many things."

"You are now talking," the Ambassador cut in. "Problems, problems, problems. Man-made problems, problems that ought not exist at all."

The two soldiers were silent, hardly knowing where the man was heading to. He resumed:

"Has it occurred to you that the hopes that were raised by independence, or even on the eve of independence, have not been realised."

"Well," Kotoka shrugged and looked at his comrade who also shrugged and said:

"Can you trust politicians? They say one thing and do another."

"But that shouldn't be the case don't you think?"

"Really," Afrifa replied. "But they always do so."

"Politics should not be all falsehood. A politician may fail to deliver on one or two electioneering promises. That is perfectly normal. But he should not contradict the principles of the platform on which he was voted. He should deliver the goods. If he makes the effort but fails in the process, we can forgive him. But he should not go all out to undercut his promises. He should move the country forward, not backward. A politician should not take innocent citizens for a ride. Worse still he should not take intelligent men for a ride. He should not despise them. He should use them, not abuse them, he should not enslave them. In fact, he should make his citizens proud to belong there where they were born."

The two officers listened and nodded but without really understanding the full import of what the diplomat was saying. The mood now was gradually becoming one of quiet reflection.

"Yes, you are right," Afrifa forced himself to say. "A good politician should move the country forward, not backwards. I agree. Eh, my man?" he turned to Kotoka who had long started nodding and as soon as he looked in his direction he admitted:

"That's true."

Ebny Whitestone put away the cigar stub, clasped his thick fingers between his gigantic thighs and began very gravely:

"When we first came here at independence," he went on, shaking his head as if recalling a bad dream with deep regret, "this great country had everything going for it: it could boast of almost the highest standard of living of any country in Africa. She had a large intellectual class, a highly efficient civil service machinery, and handsome foreign assets. Freedom-seeking Africans everywhere saw in her independence a beginning to the fulfilment of hopes for the complete liberation of the continent from colonial domination."

"Ah, you were also here during independence, Mr. Ambassador?" Kotoka stepped in excitedly.

"Like mad," the Ambassador said. "I could not have missed it for the world. And what we of the Diaspora found exhilarating and Nkrumah's first stroke of victory that made every black man hold their heads high in the skies, was that there was finally an authentic and resounding voice, uniquely African, in world affairs. If Nkrumah had done nothing else, he would always be remembered on the singular score. At no time before or since, has any African made such an impact on a Pan-African level or internationally.

"That is why we call him Osagyefo," Afrifa said with genuine pride.

Ebny Whitestone merely grinned and continued: "Here was a man who consciously and deliberately sought the role of spokesman for African people everywhere. Here was a man who consciously, successfully and consistently identified with the basic aspirations of all of African descent. And wherever he stood up to speak, one thing always stood out loud and clear, whether it was at the UNO or Commonwealth Conference, at a CPP rally or anywhere else, we looked on him as the veritable mouthpiece of the African people. Has it ever occurred to you Ghanaians to understand why we of the Diaspora responded to Nkrumah's clarion call so spontaneously and positively?"

"We are mere soldiers," Kotoka strained to tell the Ambassador, "and we are usually too busy thinking of how to defend the state than to find out or investigate motives for any government actions, be they good or bad."

There was some apparent telepathy because Afrifa seemed to be thinking along similar lines. True to their profession, these army officers learned in the army an inviolable code of conduct which demanded that they never interrupt an authority while he was talking, even if it was rubbish! But this was not rubbish! It was sense, frightfully true sense, although it lay a little bit outside the scope of their activities.

The American Ambassador seemed to have a full grasp of historical facts, something the soldiers found irresistible and fascinating and very teaching. Which was the first impression the man had wanted to create before making his point. Every word that fell out of the Ambassador's lips seemed immediately to cast a spell on the two men.

"I wonder how many Ghanaians have noticed the widening gap between all those electioneering promises which made everybody applaud and what he now practices! He must be taking Ghanaians for a ride. Otherwise, how is it possible that he will forget so soon that he was the very one sermonizing against 'bribery and corruption, both moral and factual'? Was he not the very person who professed that these vices were incompatible with the development of a wholesome society, and counselled that it 'must be stamped out if we are to achieve any progress'? Or was he merely politicking? Through a strange mixture of subterfuge and dictatorial methods, he has successfully transformed the 1957 Constitution which he had sworn to uphold, to suit his personal and party political ambition.

"That is the same messiah who has now turned round to *buy* the henchmen he was supposed to educate, just to further his own ambitions and to flatter and nurture his inflated ego, at a huge great public expense! See how he has consistently demoralised his honest following. Many of the intellectuals and the most competent administrators and educationists have been forced to flee the country. Now, instead of grooming and encouraging genuine advisers and counsellors, all we know is that he has attracted and bound to himself dishonest and incompetent 'yes men', whose only contribution to nation building is to cloud important issues, just because of the absolute power which they know their paymaster wields over everybody and everything, to cover up their own inadequacies.

"Chaos and disorganisation have begun to affect the economy and the moral and social order. He wanted to reduce everybody in Ghana to a state of prostration from which they would look up to him alone Ghana has now become a state in which everybody but the Party would be reduced to a point where only Nkrumah is the possible benefactor. This is difficult to believe of a so-called people's leader.

"Look at this affair of corruption, the canker worm that has suddenly eaten up the basic fabric of Ghanaian society. From a distance you would think he is against it, just from the way he talks. But you must look at it carefully and follow his actions step by step. His 'Dawn Broadcast' do not prove that he is really worried about integrity in public life. He would make such a broadcast against corruption, not primarily because he cared ethically about such things but mainly because he had his eyes on certain men who obstructed him in his bid for absolute power, and wanted to put fear into his underlings, because money which he knew they were collecting for the Party on contracts was not coming in, in the anticipated quantities. He would make a show taking action on charges of dishonesty levelled against those around him, but only so as to improve his own tactical position. He believes that these men 'are all the same'. He thinks it is no use dismissing, say, a minister who has been caught red-handed in a corrupt deal; his successor would do no better. So, as the ridiculous argument goes, it is better to leave the minister at his post because, having made his fortune, he is the more likely to become honest and respectable. Shame on Ghana. I say again, shame on Ghana."

14

Chapter Three

Like the crafty tempter that he was, he deliberately clouded every fact that might have justified any acts by Nkrumah which an undiscerning observer like the army officers in front of him, could easily be made to consider a failure. Historians wishing to present a balance sheet of Nkrumah's life would tell you that no politician who meant to implement a vigorous political programme would have taken the intolerance of the opposition politicians towards the CPP lightly. No politician who had the welfare of the new Ghana at heart to the degree that Nkrumah did would have ignored the secessionist activities of his political opponents; no politician could have taken the bomb that injured him so seriously at Kulungugu as a joke, or the point blank shot of the police Constable, Seth Ametewee. These and many other attempts on his life converted Nkrumah into what the western media and his detractors called a tyrant.

Thus, instead of defending the miserable deaths in the cells of Dr. J.B. Danquah and Obetsebi Lamptey (close associates of "The Big Six")as necessary evils, the West seized on it as instances of how far Nkrumah had strayed from his initial promises of liberating Africa. It was against this background that the Ambassador presented that dark picture of Nkrumah. Give a dog a bad name, so goes the saying, and hang it. He told the apparently hypnotized officers:

"Where is Nkrumah heading to? Where is he dragging Ghana to? See how he himself has crippled all efforts to realise the dreams at independence which are now fast

15

turning into a nightmare! He chased the British away and we of the Diaspora cheered because, having been imprisoned unjustly, he would be in the best position to bring freedom to the black man! But see what he has become – a complete reverse! Worse than the British. What was the point chasing away the British if he was to outdo them in their viciousness so soon and so completely? Where is the tolerance he promised? How different from the repressive British policy of detention without trial from his desire to detain his opposition rivals without trial, his so-called "Preventive Detention Acts!"

The two army officers looked at each other but remained silent.

"These actions, however politically expedient, are a painful irony. Painfully ironical because what actually endeared Nkrumah to us out there in America and the Diaspora was the fact that he did not allow his arrest and imprisonment by the British to daunt his spirits of pushing forward the struggle towards freedom for Ghana and the black race. It was that very rare transformation from prisoner to president that intrigued everybody! But see him now," the Ambassador lamented. "Things are bad and are fast getting worse. We of America and the Diaspora cannot understand why he fails to see that the wanton detention of opposition politicians undercuts his own policy of helping to liberate the rest of Africa. How does he expect the white racists in South Africa, the Rhodesian Federation and the Portuguese terrorists of Angola, Mozambique and Guinea-Bissau to mend their ways with thousands of African nationalists similarly dying by the hundreds in detention without trial?" As though reading their minds, the man went on:

"I can see that you may not be very conversant with some of these details. But you will later find that it was of the utmost importance that you know them."

He did not tell them that his presence in Ghana at that material time, and the motivating force behind all that he was doing was in response to a CIA report on Ghana, issued in December 1957, just nine months into independence, which was distributed within the America government and intelligence community. The report said:

The fortunes of Ghana – the first Tropical African country to gain independence – will have a huge impact on the evolution of Africa and Western interests there.

(To a careful reader conversant with the machinations of neo-colonialists this can only imply protecting their interests by an invitation to put an immediate halt to the activities of the upstart. As a matter of fact, Nkrumah's declaration that the independence of Ghana was meaningless unless it was followed by the total liberation of the continent, was no gimmick. Within ten years of Ghana attaining independence, thirty other African countries had followed her example. This was a development too frightening to be ignored by the imperialists and neo-colonialist masters with stakes in Africa.)

The American Ambassador only told them what he thought was necessary for him to achieve his aim.

"I am here in several capacities," he said: "I am first and foremost a U.S. diplomat; secondly I am the personal representative of the *Diasporic League of Concerned Blacks in America,* and finally I am Secretary General of a USA-based *National Association for the Advancement of Coloured People, NAACP.*"

"Never heard of that," Kotoka confessed.

"That doesn't mean that it doesn't exist," the man said.

"Well, that's not really what he means," Afrifa corrected him. The two men sat back and listened with rapt attention as the Ambassador took their minds down history lane.

"Six years before Ghana's independence, Dr Kwame visited the USA in his capacity as "Leader of Government Business" of the then Gold Coast. He was returning to

17

Lincoln University in Pennsylvania, his alma mater, at the invitation of the university's then president, Horace Mann Bond, the father of Julian Bond, chairman of the National Association for the Advancement of Coloured People, which I just mentioned that I am the Secretary General. Nkrumah was awarded an honorary Doctor of LAWS (LL.D) degree that was approved overwhelmingly by the university's board of trustees.

The officers looked on and listened wordlessly, completely lost in that welter of historical details.

"On that epoch-making day," he continued, "Nkrumah whom we were seeing for the first time was asked to give the commencement speech. In his speech he said something that almost drew tears from everybody's eyes. He invited African-Americans, Negroes if you like, to return to Ghana and help develop the country.

"'We are aiming to work under democratic principles such as exist in Britain and in the United States,' I remember him declaring to the crowd at Lincoln University. He spoke about how the Gold Coast needed technicians, machinery and capital to develop its natural resources. He had thrown a challenge at us because he said this knowing that there was much for African-Americans to do to help their ancestral country. He added that it was the intention of his Convention People's Party (CPP) to re-name the country Ghana. It was this clarion call that inspired many African-American leaders to pack their bags and baggage to return to their ancestral country.

"How did things go so bad so soon?" the Ambassador asked, looking from Kotoka's to Afrifa's face as if he had invited them for an ordinary soul-searching conversation.

Major Afrifa looked across at Kotoka and then threw a quick glance at his watch. For strategic reasons, the man was certainly taking his time to make his point. What the man was saying was certainly most educating, but they still had not made up their minds as to why he was telling them all that. Kotoka, though, knowing that the man's invitation had something sinister behind it, was beginning to show signs of nervousness: he seemed to be forcing his hands to remain still in his laps although his chin was beginning to itch from the false beard he had worn. He was trying vainly to look relaxed and bold while reminding himself not to seem too relaxed or over anxious. There were signs of nervousness also on Afrifa's hard face: lines of confusion and fear rose and fell on his forehead and jaws as if he were perpetually sucking something at once sour and sweet.

With traces of saliva bursting in foamy chains at the corners of his mouth, the Ambassador was bent on finishing his tale.

"The exodus to Ghana then began and any black man who wanted to make an impact in America and the Diaspora, had first to come to Ghana and give Nkrumah a helping hand: Dr Martin Luther King Jr. and his wife Mrs Coretta Scott King. After that visit, Dr King preached a sermon about the new Ghana titled *"Birth of a New Nation"* at his famous Dexter Avenue Baptist Church in Montgomery, Alabama. Also constituting part of the team Diaspora-based black leaders that attended the 1957 independence celebration, were such men and women like A. Phillip Randolph, the trade unionists; Congressman Adam Clayton Powell; the Nobel Prize winner and UN under-secretary-general Ralph Bunche; Lucille Armstrong (representing her husband, Louis Armstrong, the jazz legend); and the University presidents Horace Mann Bond of Lincoln and Mordecai Johnson of Howard, Dr. W.E.B. DuBois, who died here a few years ago. These were all there including those from the Caribbean nations. All in all, about 300 African-Americans came and were determined to help the Nkrumah government with various levels of involvement. This was a real revolution and every black man wanted to be a part of it."

Finally Major Afrifa could bear the filibustering no longer. He asked him wearily:

"Why are you telling us all this, Mr. Ambassador"

"Aren't you glad to know this about your president and about your country?"

Even before any of the officers responded, he pulled himself together, pulled at the cigarette, puffed out the smoke said firmly:

"Besides informing you, what I am telling you has to be said and said loudly because the dance has turned sour, that's why. Because Nkrumah is about to destroy himself, that's why. Because Nkrumah, after that magnificent start, after those giant strides, is progressively dismantling his own greatness and possibly that of All Africa, that's why. Because those organizations which I have mentioned that I represent, now believe that they have been completely misled, that they have been led down a blind alley. What began as a mere bubo has now degenerated in no time into a boil, into an abscess. The abscess has now burst and its rotten, stinking contents have over spilled into the bloodstream of Ghana, infecting the entire body politic. And there does not seem to be any remedy. It is past mending."

Kotoka stretched as if under the grip of a sudden high fever. His breathing became louder than usual, and a few bubbles of cold sweat lingered at the tip of his nose which he wiped with the back of his left hand as he stole a glance at his colleague. Afrifa was just as disturbed by the devastating metaphor of abscess the Ambassador had just employed. The two then slowly began to stare into each other's eyes before leaning forward to absorb more of the eye-opening revelations.

"And this unfortunate turn of events has not pained only those of us of the Diasporic-blacks alone who have staked so much on Ghana. African leaders of unimpeachable integrity are also feeling the ache in a manner that bodes ill for this young nation. Let me mention only one case which is near enough for you to see. You both know Dr. Nnamdi Azikiwe…"

"Of course, Mr. Ambassador. Everybody knows Zik. He is Osagyefo's very good friend."

"He was," the Ambassador corrected him.

"WAS and not IS?"

"He was his friend. And that is the point I want you to see. Dr. Azikiwe is not just an icon in African politics, but was one of the most important guests at the independence ceremony. But hear how he now regards President Nkrumah. Listen to what he had to say at Dr. Danquah's funeral." He changed his spectacles and began to read the last few lines of Dr. Nnamdi Azikiwe's fairly long Eulogy, running his finger across every word and every line:

I am sorry that Dr. Danquah died in detention camp. I wish he had been tried publicly, told what offence he was alleged to have committed, given a fair opportunity to defend himself and then either discharged or punished, depending upon the fact, whether or not his innocence has been established or his guilt proved beyond any reasonable shadow of doubt.

I am of the considered opinion that if independence means the substitution of alien rule for an indigenous tyrant, then those who struggled for the independence of former colonial territories have not only desecrated the cause of human freedom but they have betrayed their peoples.

The man bent the piece of paper he had in his hands into two with his thumb and forefinger, folded his hands and leaned back saying: "Anybody who thinks or finds this complimentary is not right upstairs."

There was a very long tense minute of silence and then Kotoka, shaking his head in utter disappointment, asked to see the document.

"I hope you do not harbour the false impression that I have faked the document.

"Not at all, not at all," Kotoka denied as he stretched his hands to receive. "How can I think so? Just that it is so bad to hear."

He then began to read the entire document to himself. That was actually the first time he was hearing about what the veteran Nigerian politician had said at the burial of Dr. Danquah.

"Very interesting," Kotoka said as he read the document. He then handed it over to his colleague. The two army officers who had been at a loss as to why they had been invited so late in the evening, were beginning to catch the drift of the man's thoughts. Every word that fell from the Ambassador's lips seemed to immediately cast a spell on the two officers as they stared on speechlessly or fidgeted in their seats. The man continued:

"The economy lies in shambles, the national debt is skyrocketing due to the squandamania of the CPP functionaries."

Here Afrifa scratched his head and smiled a bit at the term which he was hearing for the first time, but which he found so appropriate to the careless spending that they had noticed amongst the CPP officials.

"You remember that his famous 'Tighten Belts' appeal he made last year during his Christmas broadcast?"

The two officers looked at each other with guilt-ridden eyes, ashamed that they could remember so little about their President's recent Christmas speech. The man took out a bundle of newspapers from under the table and pulled out a copy of the Daily Graphic for the Christmas period containing the speech.

"Listen to your President '.... if we are to build our new industries, factories, schools, hospitals and roads, and revolutionise our agriculture as rapidly as we have been doing, we cannot afford to waste our precious earnings on luxury goods. We Ghanaians must accept for the time being the necessity to curtail the volume of consumer foods imported from abroad. The more we buy from abroad, the more we get into debt, and the less money we have for our development.' The CPP and myself have established strict control of import licences to prevent the importation of items which Ghanaians can do without..."

The man folded the newspaper and said: "Excellent economic policy, I give him full marks for thinking so. But how did this work out in practice? Bullshit empty talk. These are precisely the steps that he and his CPP have shied away from taking and were never going to take. Their major concern has been the Party and Ideology."

When he looked round his listeners were nodding. At least they knew that part of Party and Ideology.

"For the welfare of the Party President Nkrumah had seen to the establishment of a National Development Corporation (NADECO). You have heard of NADECO right?"

The soldiers nodded.

"But I am not sure that you know it to be a clearing house of Bribery into which state funds are channelled to maintain the Party. President Nkrumah had instigated the Parliament into setting up a contingency fund of some two million pounds. So you see that the only effect of the tight exchange control system was to enable ministers and CPP stalwarts, and a few small government officials, to fill their pockets with percentage commissions *extorted from hapless importers, thus forcing the prices of imported goods to leap upward.*" He raised his voice in apparent indignation when he said the last fourteen words.

The soldiers smiled again at the expression 'clearing house of bribery' and leaned forward to hear what he meant to say.

"Do you know why so many potential investors are leaving Ghana?"

The two men shrugged and then Kotoka said: "Perhaps they have finished investing."

"That's not it," the Ambassador said with a contemptuous smile. "That's not it. And do you know why so many Ghanaians are leaving Ghana?"

Afrifa smiled and said almost to himself: "Did I even know that investors and Ghanaians were leaving Ghana?"

"They are all leaving, simply because they have lost confidence in the regime."

The soldiers nodded. The Ambassador remained silent for a while as he lit a cigarette and pulled at it for some time.

"There is no follow up to any projects assigned to state corporations or enterprises. In 1961, a contract was signed for the supply of machinery and equipment by a Czechoslovakian organization for a rubber tyre factory. Of this a Ministry of Industry's progress report, issued last year stated that, although it had then been decided that this machinery and equipment must be delivered to Ghana, it was still, in 1964, lying in Czechoslovakia, where Ghana was asked to pay rent for its storage."

The two soldiers shook their heads, they did not like what they were hearing at all and wondered why it was that nobody ever made mention of it, even in conversation or rumour. The Ambassador had one more point to add:

"And there is this case too of the tannery. It was also to be built with Czechoslovakian machinery and equipment under a contract signed in 1962. It also ran into difficulties because no arrangements had been made for the buildings. The Ghana government had to ask for the shipment of further crates of machinery to be suspended when 151 had already arrived, since it was difficult to store more. I mention these to make you understand that all this waste was at the Ghanaian public expense. How was it going to be paid for? From the already overtaxed taxpayer."

Chapter Four

The Ambassador knew he was succeeding. He could see how well the case he was building up against Nkrumah was affecting them. He could sense indignation building up within them, rising to fever pitch. Everything had to be said and done within that one sitting, he reminded himself. To let them go away only partially convinced about the genuineness of his anger against Nkrumah, a veritable thorn in the side of the State's Department and America, would not do. He must work them up to the point where they would be sworn to the one purpose of seeing that the greatest favour that could be done to Ghana and even Nkrumah himself lay in getting the latter out of the way as soon as the slightest opportunity presented itself.

"On the international front, which has always been Nkrumah's forte, an area in which his influence has been most felt," the Ambassador resumed, "Nkrumah is faring even worse. In his blindness he has sacrificed the welfare of this young nation at the altar of his so-called Pan-Africanism. And even there, even there," he repeated, shaking his head in regret, "he has disappointed every hope and promise. He has proven that he is unable to establish closer and binding economic and political ties with neighbouring African countries. 'A man's reach should exceed his grasp, or what's heaven for?' goes the saying. But to hitch your wagon to a star is only an indication of an objective and has nothing to do with the means of achievement – which takes hard-working, intelligent and realist planning to achieve. Nevertheless Nkrumah has consistently failed to realise that it is the parts that make up the whole, and preferred to pursue an 'all-or-nothing' policy of a continental union government while being hostile to all attempts at sub-regional groupings or efforts. He signed a secret pact with Olympio for a Ghana-Togo union, but refused to tell either Keita or Sekou Touré with whom he had already signed another. This is double dealing.

"Perhaps or perhaps not you have heard the rumour that he was being blamed for the death of Sylvanus Olympio and Abubakar Tafawa Belewa. That aside," he waved his hand as though it was of no importance. Meanwhile he had given the officers additional food for thought. "As soldiers you should be aware of the military blunders he has dragged Ghana into…"

Afrifa tilted his head as if to search his mind for something to substantiate what the man was insinuating.

"Lumumba, finding himself in deep trouble was encouraged by Nkrumah to apply to the UN for assistance. And Nkrumah, for Christ's sake, did not stop there. He sent a contingent of Ghanaian soldiers without finding out under whose tutelage they would be performing, without finding out on whose side the UN was. He did not take time to know that the Belgians who wanted Lumumba's head were in the same camp with the UN. As a result Ghanaian troops found themselves under the command of the UN which was not exactly on favourable terms with Lumumba. The upshot of this short-sighted move was that Ghanaian troops found themselves preventing Lumumba from using his own radio at the crucial moment. And they were helpless when Lumumba was arrested and taken away to Katanga to be killed."

The two officers nodded.

"We learn every day," Afrifa mumbled inaudibly. At least they were familiar with the dubious role which the Ghanaian soldiers played in the Congo.

"Ankra and Otu had said something of the sort," Kotoka said.

The man nodded and went on:

"That aside, at its formation, the OAU had 34 members. At the Accra Conference last year, in only under two years, the number has dwindled to 28…"

"That is news to us," Kotoka remarked looking at his colleague who also nodded.

"But that is what has happened."

"And why so?"

"Because of your Nkrumah's short-sighted policy of freedom fighters. Members of the French bloc – Upper Volta, Ivory Coast, Cameroon, Dahomey, Niger and Togo boycotted it. Why would a man gifted with such a vision of independence be unable to see that the umbilical cord between France and its overseas territories has never been cut, and that by providing shelter to rebels who are fighting tooth and nail to overthrow the French-run regimes he was directly subverting those governments?

"And in the domain of freedom fighters where he is so vocal, he leaves people completely confused. And why am I saying this? Because his mistakes are legion, even there. For instance, in 1962 when Nelson Mandela made his famous trip *incognito* across Africa, during which he addressed the Addis Ababa Conference of the Pan-African Freedom Movement in Africa, South of the Sahara, he did visit Ghana…"

Kotoka looked across at Afrifa and bit his lower lip with his teeth, suppressing the temptation to laugh at his complete ignorance of what the man was saying.

"Yes, that's what happened," the Ambassador said. "But the bad part is that he could not meet Nkrumah. He failed to meet Nkrumah at a time when the Ghanaians were under the influence of the Pan-Africanist Congress of South Africa."

"But why could he not meet Nkrumah, Mr. Ambassador?" Kotoka enquired.

"Because of the dumb stooges he had around him. On Nelson Mandela's own admission, when he asked to meet the Osagyefo, Ako Adjei, his sycophantic foreign minister, told him to wait for a fortnight, during which a conference was due to open in Accra, and 'everyone would get a chance to see Nkrumah'. Just imagine something like that!"

"And so he finally didn't meet Nkrumah?" Afrifa asked.

"But that's the point I am making. He could not wait long, and left. When he got to Nigeria, the Sardauna of Sokoto and Prime Minister Balewa were very nice to him. He said they gave the African National Congress £10,000."

Here he smiled to himself, shook his head in disappointment and concluded:

"This is certainly one of the supreme ironies of Ghanaian history: that its leader, who proclaimed African liberation from the rooftops, and regarded the leaders of Nigeria as "reactionaries", lost the chance of meeting the most famous freedom fighter the continent has produced; the man who was to bring about the greatest feat of liberation in Africa's history. And that in Mandela's eyes, at any rate, the Sardauna of Sokoto and Alhaji Abubakar Tafawa Balewa should rank above Nkrumah in terms of the support they gave to his struggle. That's why I say he seems to be dancing a dance which only he alone understands. He is confused and as such has left his ardent and more reflective supporters like ourselves, even more confused. This is a very sad commentary on the life of this once so promising leader.

"He has taken Ghana out of the Commonwealth. He plans to set up an OAU High Command at the helm of which he has already placed the Ghanaian army. You should be aware of this, at least," he threw his open hands in the direction of the two officers.

They nodded and said: "we know some of it," Afrifa countered.

"This is a far cry from the Nkrumah the Diasporic-blacks hailed to the skies not so long ago. This is madness. Or at least every step that he has taken draws him nearer and nearer the lunatic fringe of international relations. You of the military know only too well that it can only spell suicide when an army engages in wars on so many fronts – the Portuguese in Mozambique, Portuguese Guinea, Angola, and South West Africa of Namibia; all at once when one does not have the necessary resources to win even one battle. Can the Ghanaian Army fight the Rhodesia of Ian Smith, no matter how wrong Smith is in his Unilateral Declaration of Independence?"

"No way," the two men said.

"Can Ghana fight South Africa?"

"No way, no way," the two men said.

At this the man shook his head sadly and said:

"Definitely. Even if the Ghanaian army was that powerful, it would be foolhardy to confront all these so-called enemies at once. President Nkrumah has run out of positive ideas. In economic terms, we say the law of diminishing return has set in."

"I am not sure we understand what the Ambassador means," Kotoka spoke for both of them.

"I won't be surprised if you do not," he said. "Every step he takes now only serves to produce the opposite and unintended result. That's what I mean."

Kotoka supported his right jaw in his right palm and stared on.

"Ghana is now fast becoming the laughingstock of Africa. Where did things go wrong? Tell me gentlemen."

Kotoka indicated that he had something to say.

"Am listening, officer," the Ambassador called on him.

"As for me I think it is because Osagyefo is his own adviser. He does not take advice from anybody. He takes every decision himself. And then he doesn't like to be criticised. Whenever somebody publishes any article in the press that points out the wrong in something he or the CPP has done, he orders us to arrest the person. So the press never blames him again. It only praises him."

"But that is wrong," the Ambassador said.

The two officers shrugged as if to say "But there it is, what else can we do?" Afrifa ran his hands over his face and cleared his throat, indicating that he had something to say.

"Go on," the Ambassador said in his throat.

"Mr. Ambassador, I think our problem stems from how God made us Ghanaians."

"How do you mean?"

"You see we Ghanaians are made very docile and cowardly. We always fear to criticise something or other people openly, most of all people or situations we do not hate, especially people in power. We very easily resign and sit back and say, 'God knows why He has done this or that to us.' That is our nature. So when you see Ghanaians sitting like dumb and deaf people while heavy taxes are crushing them, while bribery and corruption is being practised by everybody in the Nkrumah government, it should not surprise you. Although everybody knows that Nkrumah does not take advice, that he is always his own only adviser, they sit around him and continue to worship him. There are always Ghanaians very prepared to carry out his orders without question; there are Ghanaian judges always prepared to give him the kind of judgments that they know will please him. That's Ghana, Mr. Ambassador.

"The people we were all looking up to, have failed us. What do we as soldiers know about drawing up a constitution? Look at this one of 1960 which so many people are complaining about, that Osagyefo has put into his pocket. It was drawn up by university lecturers and professors, economists and politicians. They all saw that there was something seriously wrong with it…"

"And they went on to apply it, why?" the Ambassador queried.

"And they went on to apply it just for the same reason that I have given. Nobody was anxious to stand up and say 'No' to it. And also, many of the university staffs at that time were made up largely of expatriates. Some of them seeing that their Ghanaian counterparts were silent also preferred to resign rather than speak out against things which Ghanaians were not complaining about. That, I think is what has brought us to this point."

"You can never be more correct in your assessment of your people," the Ambassador admitted. "Now you see that Nkrumah is a product of the Ghanaian people. Nkrumah were no lion were Ghanaians not sheep. There is a saying that he who makes himself a sheep must expect to be eaten by wolves. But all is not lost, at least not yet, not from the way we see it," he said with a mocking smile playing at the corners of his mouth. He put away the cigarette stub, then sat up at akimbo and said to the two men.

"I find what you are saying very interesting. I find it interesting in that you have pointed accusing fingers at everybody else – the egomania, the sycophancy and tactlessness of his followers, the judiciary, the intellectuals and the indolence of the Ghanaian populace. But, and I am very glad it turned out that way, you have not accused yourselves the soldiers. Look at what happened to Ankra upon his return from the Congo. Was it his fault that the mission to the Congo flopped?"

The two men shook their heads in denial. The Ambassador went on. He was not only a quintessential spellbinder but a rabble-rouser of the first order. As he had expected, the reference to Ankra had struck the two officers at the point of keenest interest – military morale. Both men remembered how upon return from the Congo, Ankra had been dehumanised. After firing him, Nkrumah gave the impression that if he came and begged he would be pardoned. Ankra did come begging, crying and crawling on his knees before him. And while the other officers looked on in shock, Nkrumah put his foot on his head in triumph.

"There, they say they are soldiers. See how they beg and cry before me," Nkrumah said afterwards in triumphant glee, obviously unaware that sane people do not behave like that. War veterans should be honoured, not humiliated," the Ambassador resumed with fiery eloquence. "How long ago was it since you had your pay raise?"

"Pay what?" the two officers asked, visibly incensed and sad at the disclosures.

"Pay raise, salary increase. How long ago?"

The two men laughed and Afrifa said:

"Ghana is a poor country…."

"Ghana is not a poor country. It is Nkrumah who has decided to make it seem so."

"Anyway, we do not have salary increase," Afrifa pointed out.

Ebny Whitestone smiled a knowing smile and then asked:

"What's your salary like? I know how personal this is, but let me just ask, how much do you earn?"

"About 2000."

"Two thousand what?"

"Two thousand New Cedis."

"How much is that in *real* money?"

"You mean-eh?" Kotoka stepped in.

"How much is that in dollars?"

When the conversion was made Whitestone exclaimed "Jeeez!" and then gave a long deprecating laugh. Then still shaking with laughter he remarked:

"That's peanuts, that's hamburger money. That's not even enough to take care of an automobile."

The two officers shrugged helplessly but remained silent.

"How many pairs of uniforms do you each possess?"

"Two," the men said. "Our daily wear and then our ceremonial wear," Kotoka added.

"How often do they replace them?"

Again the two men laughed. They could hardly recall when they last had a new pair of uniforms supplied.

"Or until they are worn threadbare?"

The two men nodded smiling and shaking their heads in apparent shame.

"Now you are being called upon to be part of an action which will place you in a position to decide your salary, to decide how many pairs of uniforms you will need a week. As I was saying before this salary thing came up, you have not accused the police. By the grace of God Nkrumah has not tampered with the one body which alone has the powers to put an end to this mess. In many underdeveloped countries where rulers are anxious to perpetuate their reigns, they promote grossly incompetent people from their own villages to positions of power so that it becomes impossible for the army to intervene and set things in order when the situation reaches breaking point.

"You do not have that excuse. You," he pointed at Afrifa, "you are an Ashanti. And you," he pointed at Kotoka, "you are an Ewe. The head of the police," he scratched his head and searched his mind for the name.

"You mean Harlley…"

"Thanks. Yes, Harlley, J.W. Harlley. You are both Ewes. There is really no problem between Ewes and Ashantis, as far as my limited knowledge of Ghanaian geo-politics goes. As a matter of fact, my sources tell me that there is an understanding between the Ewes and the Ashantis which Nkrumah has always feared. How many Nzimas of rank do you find in either the police or the army?"

"Very few," Kotoka responded.

"You can count them by the fingers of one hand," the Ambassador said. With indignation still swelling in the breasts of the officers, the Ambassador raised the issue of Nkrumah's malignancy. He retold the story of the celebrated case of a trumped up charge that was made against two of Nkrumah's opponents whose popularity was threatening his security - the celebrated case of Amponsah and Apaloo. When it came to the attention of Nkrumah in 1958 that some members of the Opposition United Party were planning a coup against the Government, Nkrumah lent assistance by hatching a spurious plot to involve the principals-R.R. Amponsah, M.K. Apaloo and J.K. Mensah. He thereby succeeded in obtaining a most dubious conviction against these and others on the grounds that they were 'engaged in a conspiracy to carry out at some future date in Ghana an act for an unlawful purpose revolutionary in character', and to use this case to secure all the repressive legislation he wanted, as well as to detain these three and others he disliked or was worried about.

It would be interesting to go into some of the details of this case. As soon as Nkrumah became aware through his security channels that Amposah and Apaloo were planning his overthrow, he embarked on a remarkable plan. Major Awhaitey, one of the most senior Ghanaians in the Army and the only Ghanaian who at that time held independent Command, was contacted by imposters, acting under Nkrumah's orders, who represented themselves to him as Amponsah and Apaloo. These two asked Major Awhaitey to organize, through the use of military personnel, the assassination of the Prime Minister when he was leaving for India two days later. Nkrumah had hoped, perhaps, that Awhaitey would report this message to the appropriate authorities so that Apaloo and Amponsah would be arrested; but he did not do so. Rather he chose to confide in a brother-officer. Awhaitey was later contacted again and told to meet both Amponsah and Apaloo at the now famous 'T-junction' formed by the Accra, Tema and Burma Camp roads, to discuss their plans for action. In the meantime Amponsah had been asked on the telephone by someone calling himself Apaloo, to meet the caller at the T-junction. At the appointed time, Amponsah went to the T-junction and, while he was waiting there was arrested. Apaloo was later arrested, and Major Awhaitey was court-martialled.

The Government appointed a Commission of Enquiry that consisted of Gilbert Granville Sharp, an English QC, then serving as a Justice of Appeal in Ghana; Mr. Justice M.A. Charles, a member of the Commonwealth Overseas Legal Service then serving as a Senior Magistrate, and Sir Tsibu Darku, a former paramount chief, who for eight years, before the 1951 Constitution had been a member of the Governor's Executive Council.

The Commission was unanimous in finding that R.R. Amponsah and M.K. Apaloo had, since June 1958, been engaged in a conspiracy to carry out 'at some future date in Ghana an act for an unlawful purpose revolutionary in character' and that these two had been engaged together in the purchase of military outfit and equipment, which they had transferred to the Republic of Togo. They found however that Lieutenant Amenyah, the originator of the report on which the Police and Army had acted, was, on the whole, an unsatisfactory witness. He gave false evidence when he stated on oath that he had never been a member of the CPP, and the Commissioners agreed that it would be dangerous for them to act on his evidence when any part of it was not supported by other testimony or circumstances. Major Awhaitey, they agreed had not been telling 'the whole truth'. However Justice Charles and Sir Tsibu were agreed on the fact that Amponsah, Apaloo and his brother Mensah Anthony were 'engaged in a conspiracy to assassinate the Prime Minister, Dr. Kwame Nkrumah, and to carry out a *coup d'état'*. Mr. Granville Sharp, in a minority report on this particular issue, held that after the second week in November 1958 R.R. Amponsah and M.K. Apaloo were no longer associated in a conspiracy to carry out a *coup d'état*, and that they had abandoned their revolutionary projects when they learned on November 20 that the Police knew they had purchased military accoutrement in the United Kingdom. He held also that persons unknown had secured Amponsah's presence at the Labadi Road T-junction at 7 p.m. on December 19, and put Apaloo to the trouble of searching for Amponsah at that place after Amponsah had been arrested. The Government accepted the majority report and made the most of it when they came later to introduce restrictive measures.

Nkrumah must have learned much from this commission of enquiry and had high hopes of what he could expect from trials of this kind in future. There is no doubt that his expectations when Adamafio, Cofie Crabbe and Ako Adjei came to trial, and the fury he wrought on the Supreme Court justice when they failed to give him the verdict he expected in that case, stemmed from the ease with which a majority decision was given in his 'favour' in the Amponsah-Apaloo case.

When he came to the end of that recital and lighted another cigarette, Afrifa could not conceal his admiration. "The Ambassador seems to know more about us than we Ghanaians," he confessed frankly. "It is like you are the Ghanaian and we the strangers listening to you."

"Thanks for the compliment. But it is only natural that I should know all this, otherwise I would not have been sent out here to help you correct these monumental mistakes. I needed to talk from a position of strength."

The two officers could feel the scales falling from their own eyes as they began to see themselves and the Ghanaian situation differently, the same way that the Ambassador seemed to have seen it all along.

"You have the yam and the knife. The survival of this nascent democracy, this star of Africa lies squarely on your shoulders. It is now up to you three to make or mar. We need to talk to Harlley too…"

"No, don't worry about him. He is my man," Kotoka said. "We were both born and bred in the Volta Region. We went to school together. We will talk to him."

"You will?"

"Sure."

"Great."

Chapter Five

The word that hung in the air, unexpressed, but underlying everything that the Ambassador said was *Coup D'état*. The crafty diplomat carefully avoided mentioning the word. He seemed only bent on *stopping* Nkrumah, or *saving* Ghana from further shame, or at worst, *saving Nkrumah from himself*. It was as if there was some other way of putting an end to the deteriorating situation of things than a violent seizure of power. He was careful not to use the word bluntly because he was not very sure that they would buy his idea so easily. He was prepared to retract with *sincere* apologies, anything he had said regarding violence if the people demurred. He would then have told them: "I am not suggesting that the army takes over. I am simply drawing your attention to a bad situation so that you too should be as aware of it as the other friendly nations and organisations." But he seems to have won them over and so nothing stopped him from coming out plain.

   .   "Remember, we are not making heroes of you," he said as if the idea of a coup d'état had already been agreed upon. "We are making you what you really should be – saviours of Ghana. When a great man like Nkrumah starts undoing his own handiwork, he should be halted, for his own good. Bear in mind that you of the police and military are the military conscience of your country. Where the politicians and people are apparently powerless or have been forced into that position of powerlessness by a blind despot, a concise and swift intervention is the only way out by which a fresh lease of life can be given."

At this juncture he thought it most appropriate to produce his trump card: he rose and went into his inner chamber and soon returned with a brief case which he placed on the table in front of the two men who now seemed paralysed by the man's' persuasiveness. For once they thought it was a brand of hand guns.

"What's this?" the two men asked at once, their eyes popping out of their sockets in childlike excitement.

"Money, dollars, a gift from your friendly nations and friendly organisations to help you through this difficult task."

"How much do we have in here, Mr. Ambassador?"

"Twelve million dollars. Count it to make sure."

"No need," Kotoka said.

They took in a very long, deep breath, simultaneously. Afrifa stared at the open brief case, took one bundle of $1000 bills, weighed it in his right hand and then carefully placed it back.

"It's genuine money," the Ambassador told him. "The kind of business you are being called upon by the international bodies to carry out cannot be done with bare hands. It will involve ferrying troops from one part of the country to another on the spur of the moment. They will have to be fed. You will not have to ask Nkrumah to give you the key to the treasury so that you withdraw money for use."

The two officers laughed and the Ambassador switched a grin, on and off.

"You will need to sponsor trips of your new ambassadors to various corridors of power to explain your actions. So you see that you must be self-sufficient," he continued, "until things settle down well enough for you to discuss financial matters with your new minister of finance...

Afrifa leaned back while his colleague gave his eyes a feast for a whole minute and then leaning towards him, said in a low voice and with the same child-like glee and surprise:

"Charley, this thing is no joke-oh!"

The Ambassador nodded with satisfaction at the result of his handiwork. With the money secure in their hands, and with their heads spinning with ideas as to how they would spend the money, the officers decided at once that Nkrumah must be guilty. And the more they imagined what a change that would make to their future, the more guilty Nkrumah seemed to become. Even if he were a saint, they would have to concoct a case against him, if only to own that money. Luckily for them, they did not even need to concoct any evidence. They only needed to be able to tell the truth the way the Ambassador had told it, and then they would be rich forever! They would hand over to civilians as soon as possible, and go into early retirement, set up cattle ranches, send their kids abroad, set up businesses in the names of their relatives; they would go to Europe any time they wanted with their girlfriends just to enjoy life.

Chapter Six

Looking round the room and along the walls apprehensively, as if to reassure himself that nobody else was listening, Kotoka threw his eyes over the Ambassador's head and saw Kwame Nkrumah's picture. It appeared to have sprung on to the wall from almost nowhere. Actually it had been hanging there all along, to the left of that of President Lyndon B. Johnson, but it was that feeling of guilt of what he and his colleague had consented to do to him that had made Kotoka now aware of its presence. It seemed to stare at Kotoka so accusingly and persistently that the latter ventured to voice his apprehensions and reservation about the impending deed.

"Mr. Ambassador," he began, "we understand what you are saying. But we want you to understand what kind of creature we are talking about. Nkrumah is not an ordinary human being."

"How do you mean?"

Kotoka took a rather long time to explain his point. The reason being that he (and the same could be said of Afrifa), had grown up hearing tall tales about Nkrumah. Accounts of Nkrumah's interests in spirituality were an open book. In his well-researched but blistering account of Nkrumah's rise and fall – KWAME NKRUMAH: ANATOMY OF AN AFRICAN DICTATORSHIP, Peter Omari has pointed out that:

He[Nkrumah] is believed to have studied spiritualism, also it is said that during his stay in the United States he was a freemason. Freemasonry influenced him deeply. He fasted regularly on Fridays, and allowed himself time for meditation every day. Only his vanity led to his well-known fasting and meditation for 'Ghana and Africa' near his birthplace at Nkroful in 1965 being so widely publicized. But he genuinely believed in the 'spirit' world, and carefully observed certain taboos. He would never travel on Tuesdays and, before undertaking any journey, he had to find out whether or not it was propitious to do so. On his last journey to Perking, he left Ghana on a Tuesday. But, if he believed so deeply that man's actions are governed and influenced by consistent spiritual forces, why did he not seem to believe in objective truth: right and wrong? Perhaps he believed that one fasts and meditates for strength and insight in order to overcome one's enemies in a world full of strife; it is also probable that he came to think of himself as the incarnation of some spiritual force. After 1960, Nkrumah became deeply involved in spiritualism and relied on fetishes, especially following the many attempts on his life. He consulted oracles on every conceivable topic. Often sitting in front of Flagstaff House was an assortment of fetish priests and soothsayers from Ghana, Guinea and elsewhere, while others did their work by remote control.

But the story that readily came to Kotoka's mind was the one all his schoolmates would always remember. He remembered his old teacher, Yaasei, who virtually adored Nkrumah. He was never tired of telling them that Kwame Nkrumah, was one of the "Big Six" leaders of the UGCC – Ako Adjei, Akufor Addo, J.B. Danquah, Obetsebi Lamptey, William Ofori Atta and Kwame Nkrumah – who really knew how to combat the British.

"You can see from his photographs that he doesn't part his hair," Yaasei would say. "He also prefers to wear a *fugu* from the Northern Territories [rather] than the English suits the others like to wear. So, you see, he is against anything that is not African. He wants us to be ourselves. But above all, *waben*!"

They would cheer and drum so loudly when Yaasei said this that he would have to warn them to restrain themselves. Now '*waben*' is a term that has no English equivalent. Literally it means "He's been boiled through and through.' But figuratively, it means , 'He's versed in juju or African magic.

They were impressed when Yaasei said Nkrumah dabbled in these things because they all believed that in Nzema, where Nkrumah came from, indigenous religious rites took place that enabled people to perform supernatural feats. Secretly, most of them entertained fantasies of one day obtaining '*Nzema bayie*' (Nzema witchcraft) which would empower us to make lots of money, make any pretty girl fall in love with them, or punish a senior prefect who bullied them. And here was their teacher, custodian of all truth, confirming for us that Nkrumah, an Nzema man, was, indeed, "well-medicined". Ho, they loved the man!

Yaasei would go on, "When the British arrested The Big Six [leaders of the UGCC] after the February 1948 riots [in the wake of the "boycott Campaign" launched by Nii Kwabena Bonne, Chief of Osu Alata in Accra] the British deported the leaders to a remote prison in the north. There, the British tried to poison The Big Six. But each time they sent poisoned food to one of them, Nkrumah would use his Nzema witchcraft to turn himself into a cat, go into the cell, and overturn the poisoned food, before it could be eaten. He would then go into the bush to fetch bananas and other wholesome fruits for them to eat!"

So all of Nkrumah's successes the story went, were no accident and could very easily be understood only in the light of his magical powers – from his triumphant release from prison after the CPP won the general election of February 8 1951; his immediate elevation to Leader of Government Business (February 12 1951, and later Prime Minister (March 21 1952), President, 1957 and miraculous delivery from bomb attacks. Kotoka did not think the case was strong enough to be presented to the Ambassador. So when the latter asked him to explain he simply shrugged and said:

"He has protection on all sides. Both natural and supernatural. He behaves like a partridge."

"Partridge? How is that?"

It was Afrifa who clarified the expression.

"Excellency, that's an expression from Akan folklore. A man is said to have the instincts of a partridge when he can smell danger from a distance and can always escape before it happens."

He looked at his colleague and the man nodded in support of the explanation.

"Yes, Osagyefo is that kind of person. He takes no chances when it comes to a matter of protecting himself. Look at the fortifications around his residence, the Flagstaff House. He has recruited Russian mercenaries and other instructors who had trained his own bodyguards and who are also engaged in organising the President's Own Guard Regiment. He has bullet-proof limousines in which he can always melt away from a tight situation.

"As for medicines he is always attended by three doctors at once, never one because he does not trust any of them. He never allows himself to be injected with a drug except in the presence of at least one other doctor. He must be told the name of the drug in advance, shown the ampoule containing the drug with the label for the approval and the approval of other attending physicians. He will not take a pill or capsule unless a new box is brought and opened in his presence.

"Then, on top of all these precautions, he has also surrounded himself with juju men."

"With what?"

"With witch doctors. Excellency, have you heard of Ambrose Yankey?"

"The Minister who replaced Adamafio after the …."

46

"Yes, Excellency."

"Of course I know him, what about him?"

"You know him well?"

"Well I know that he replaced Adamafio as his chief of security. And that he has been very instrumental in causing numerous unjustified arrests of political opponents."

"That man is not a real minister. He was selling fish at Takoradi market not so long ago. We don't even know whether he can read or write anything really sensible."

"Then how did he manage to occupy such an important position in the government?"

The two men laughed derisively and then the officer went on:

"Initially Yankey was usually sent by Osagyefo to Guinea to consult with *Kankan Nyame*."

"And who was this *Nyame* fellow?"

"*Kankan Nyame* means the '*kankan* god'. Nkrumah will not travel unless he has consulted Yankey. Yankey must tell him that nothing evil will befall him, otherwise he will not travel."

The Ambassador smiled to himself and said: "The fellow must have a lot of influence on the President."

"Too much," Afrifa said. "He directs the affairs of this country, and we know it."

"A kind of Ghanaian version of Rasputin," the man said.

The two men simply nodded, since they had no knowledge of what he meant. Finally Kotoka asked falteringly:

"What is a Ras...Ras...tupi?"

The Ambassador smiled at the officer's ignorance and then said:

"Actually, Rasputin, or Gregory Rasputin, to give him his full name, was a religious charlatan who found himself by accident in the court of Tsar Nicholas II of Russia on the eve of the Bolshevik Revolution. I am sure you know of the Bolshevik Revolution?"

Afrifa shook his head in denial while Kotoka nodded doubtfully.

"Anyway, this crook was able to use some mystical powers to do what no physician in all Russia could do: he successfully treated the heir to the Russian throne of a bleeding problem called Haemophilia. From then he won the heart of the queen, Alexandria. And he who wins the heart of the queen has won the heart of the King! He soon had so much influence on the Tsar and the queen that he could even cause ministers to be appointed or dismissed."

"Exactly, Excellency," the two men answered together.

"Exactly what?" the Ambassador asked, a bit confused.

"That is exactly what Yankey is now doing," Kotoka said. "Big big Ministers bribe him in order to remain in Osagyefo's favour. And then what happened to our reputing man?"

"What else did you expect?"

"Members of the Tsar's court who felt outraged that the destiny of the nation should lie with such a rascal killed him."

"Oooh," the two men shouted.

"Of course, what did you expect? And then they killed Nicholas and Alexandria and all their children. It was a terrible thing. But that is what happens if an individual thinks he can fool all the people all the time. The rubbish just had to end somewhere."

"Thank God for Ghana'oh. Yankey has even given Osagyefo a calendar for travel."

"What kind of calendar?"

"There are days on which Osagyefo does not travel. He does not travel on Tuesdays, for instance and things like that."

"But do you give any credence to such superstition?"

Chapter Seven

The two men exchanged meaningful glances. They did not confess that it was thanks to sorcery that they had risen to such heights in their professions. They did not even think of mentioning that each of them sitting there consulted witch doctors every month for protection, or that they had concealed round their necks and waists, protective charms. Rather, Afrifa said:

"As Africans, as Ghanaians, Excellency, we believe in black magic. We believe in juju. We have seen Nkrumah do things which we think can only be done by a man of supernatural powers."

The Ambassador nodded several times and said: "Gentlemen, I have no control over what you believe or do not believe in. But it will be foolhardy to engage him in a pitched battle, what with the Russian mercenaries and the like. The neatest way is to get him out of the way before you take any action. If he is out of the country…"

"Osagyefo cannot leave, Excellency. *Kankan Nyame*, or Yankey, or some other god will warn him and he will remain." Afrifa said and Kotoka concurred.

"From what you two are saying it seems to me that you have only a one-sided view of Nkrumah…"

"One-sided? We know everything about him."

"You do not, and let me tell you why I say so."

"We are listening," the two men said.

"Good. Do you know that Nkrumah is a political animal?"

"At least we know that he is a politician. And we have said that he has the instincts of an animal, a partridge. If that is what you mean," Kotoka put in.

"That's not quite what I mean. You need to know that all those oracles and supernatural powers he seeks are for a single overriding purpose – to keep him alive so that he can realise his terrible political dream which is fast turning into a nightmare for us all. You have also to know that Nkrumah is an egomaniac and he will not hesitate to submit to any line of action that will boost his image as the foremost politician of all time."

The two men gave impressive nods. The Ambassador was sounding more and more convincing, especially now that there was money in their pockets. He was now talking to the converted. But they had some fears as to how to cause Nkrumah to travel out of the country. Ebny Whitestone had a ready answer:

"Good, and as I see it, one of the actions he would do everything to realise is to lead a peace mission to Hanoi. That lies in the heart of his political agenda right now. Nothing will please his ego more than the fact that he, Kwame Nkrumah of Africa, single-handedly caused the War in Vietnam to end. If you have any doubts in your minds about what I am saying, bring me that his supernatural Calendar along with all the gods that line the West African coast. Let them say he cannot travel on such and such a day. Let me also present him a ticket to travel to Hanoi with total guarantee of safety, on that day and let's see which one he will yield to."

The two men laughed and nodded and the Ambassador laughed too. He told Kotoka to put the brief case away. Kotoka put it first between his legs, then he placed it against the left side of the arm chair in which he was sitting before transferring it to the right side. Always on his guards, he leaned towards Afrifa and mumbled something in the vernacular which made the two of them laugh heartily. When they looked across at Ebny Whitestone the man felt a bit uneasy and wanted to know what the man had said.

"It's an Akan joke about crossing the river," Afrifa said.

"What about it? What does it say?" he pressed on.

"Just a tribal joke," Kotoka said and then the two of them tried to tell it at the same time and then stopped. The Ambassador pointed to Kotoka to tell it. With a smile still playing at the corners of his mouth he said:

"My man talked of leaving one in the middle of a river."

The Ambassador tilted his head and then asked:

"Is that it?"

"That's it."

"I don't get the joke," the man confessed.

The man explained:

"You see there is this Akan saying that if you won't ferry a person to the other side, then don't even carry him at all. What they mean is that you do not take a person to the middle of the river and ask him to go down because you have done a lot already."

The Ambassador nodded and now smiled. Then he enquired:

"So you are afraid we will abandon you in the middle of things?"

"Something like that," Kotoka admitted frankly. "We are mere soldiers," he said. "We are not politicians who know how to hold rallies and explain policies to market women and students or civil servants."

"Have no fears. You just do your part. We will be with you all the way. And as I said, nobody expects you to become economists or philosophers or technocrats overnight. Everybody knows you are soldiers whose places are in the barracks. Your role will be just to liberate your people from bondage, stay on just long enough to permit all those technocrats whom Nkrumah's heavy-handedness and blindness had driven underground to re-emerge. And then, you hand over to a civilian government. You don't need to implement any policies or even formulate them. You will find that just making sure that Nkrumah does not return to power will take a long time. That in itself is a very great achievement for this country. And you cannot be doing that while formulating and implementing economic, social and political programs."

Chapter Eight

The money started worrying the two soldiers from the very first night that they received it. Their first problem was how to conceal it, even for that night. But it did not take them long to agree that it should be kept in a large discarded carton, in the boot of Kotoka's vehicle and parked at the army barracks. Many possibilities were considered and dismissed as to what to do with it after that first night. Finally it was decided that it would be safest to hide it with a certain Auntie Benedicta, Kotoka's aunt at Takoradi. One thing was certain, the money was not going to be put in any bank because it ran the risk of creating suspicion. It was not to be banked abroad, for the same reason. They would give it to Aunt Benedicta for safe keeping.

They would leave the money with her; they would take out $1,000,000, keep $400,000 each and give $200,000 to the Chief of Police who was to be co-opted as soon as possible. How each of them spent that particular sum of money was of no real consequence, but they reminded themselves that they needed to proceed most prudently. The main strategy at that point was to start preparing the ground for the D-Day. When that moment arrived, they agreed that success would depend on having the soldiery and the police force on their side. For that reason, it was important that they started by systematically winning the admiration, love and respect of both the senior as well as the junior officers.

Each of them was aware that the exchange rates were very low in the banks, so they converted the dollars into New Cedis by sending agents to Lome-Togo to do the exchange in the black market. That gave them about ten times the value of the money they would have got if they put it directly into the bank, that meant ten times the amount of money the American Ambassador had in mind when he offered them the initial lump sum. They were each instantly rich, very rich, rich beyond their wildest dreams.

But the wooing of their subordinates by acts of altruism was to be done in such a way as not to draw attention to their new found wealth. For example, Afrifa said he would celebrate his birthday in grand style: he would invite both the senior and junior officers and give them a treat. In the service too, an outward sign of patriotism must become part and parcel of his life. He would, from time to time, give the soldiers under his charge lectures on solidarity, love of fatherland, dedication, obedience and the like. All this was so that when the moment came for him to call on their loyalty, the soldiers would not doubt his sincerity and the genuineness of his motives. They would simply believe that a man who was so generous and who demonstrated so much concern for the fatherland and his fellow comrades-in-arms, could only mean well if he had decided to take up arms against the establishment. Kotoka bought the idea *in toto*

After taking out the $1,000,000 and sharing out as agreed upon, they decided to undertake the trip to Takoradi. The rest of the money was divided into two and carefully concealed in two small tin boxes. Each of the two tin boxes was wrapped in papers and clothing before being put in a larger box. Two portmanteaux were then purchased into which each of the boxes was put before being locked with keys and then bound round and round with a thick wire, such that it was not possible for anybody to tamper with the contents without really damaging the portmanteaux.

"But I must warn you, Charley," Kotoka told his companion. "My aunt is a diehard CPP. Osagyefo is her idol, her God. She is very intolerant of anybody and anything that is not in praise of Osagyefo. She used to compose songs when we were young in which she said Osagyefo is omnipresent, omniscient, omnipotent, ubiquitous, and things of the sort. Although it is said that we of the armed forced should be neutral when it comes to politics and political parties, she knows that I am a fan of Nkrumah, having grown up in her care in Ho."

He did not tell his colleague that it was through her influence in the party that he, Kotoka had risen so rapidly to the rank of a commanding officer. Nor did he tell Afrifa that she had the sole monopoly of stitching and supplying women's uniforms for the Party in the entire Western Zone. That was not a contract that was given to just any kind of person. You must be a real dyed-in-the-wool supporter of Osagyefo. Kotoka simply said:

"So we must be careful about how we introduce the matter to her."

"Are we going to tell her that it is money for the overthrow of her idol?" Afrifa asked, smiling.

"I was wondering," Kotoka said.

"It will be madness for her even to be made to guess that it is money."

"I have an idea," Kotoka said with sudden exhilaration, and then went on to explain: They would tell her that with so many threats on Nkrumah's life, he has been advised to be alert. What they were carrying were weapons which had been entrusted into their care by Nkrumah's Chief of Security. They had been instructed to hide them and in the event of a sudden attack on the President and all weapons seized by the enemies of the state, these could be used to fight and defend the President. Afrifa bought the idea instantly, but added that she must be told never to release the parcels to any one person alone. The two of them must be present. Kotoka too bought the idea.

***

The trip to Takoradi was duly undertaken. Auntie Benedicta was a prototypical Amazon: a heavily built woman approaching seventy, a former school teacher and headmistress, she was taller than each of the two of them with arms that looked larger than their thighs and, to confirm what Kotoka had said about her allegiance to the Party, she was wearing the most recent version of the Party uniform with a picture of Nkrumah and Lumumba shaking hands and smiling on it. The dress reached right to her broad feet. She was very glad to see them and listened very attentively to their reason for coming and then agreed to be of help. Her house was adorned with effigies of Nkrumah. There was even a picture in which Nkrumah was shaking hands with her and another in which he was awarding her a medal for meritorious service to the Party.

She looked sincerely disturbed when she learned that there was even the slightest fear that something could ever happen to her idol. For one thing, she knew, or believed that Osagyefo was invulnerable, indestructible. But the very thought, however unimaginable it could be, sounded hurtful in her ears. However, she was especially glad that her son was playing such an important role in the protection of her ideological father. The two boxes were given to her and she promised to abide by the suggestions they had made.

And then the two officers returned, each to his own post while they continued to plan. Junior officers or police sent on quite simple errands were tipped very generously. Those who were sent to work in their homes returned with news of very rare generosity and continued to bless their families and wish them well. In their various stations, junior police officers as well as soldiers in hospital were visited and given surprised packages by Kotoka, Afrifa or Harlley. Invitations for family events were stretched to CPP stalwarts, all of whom were treated with very great respect. There wasn't very much money in circulation, to say the least, and so everybody invited was just too glad to be part of the event. News of the men's generosity as well as their overt declaration for the Party inevitably reached Nkrumah's ears. He not only felt flattered but was glad to see that the soldiers' sympathies were actually with the regime.

Chapter Nine

On October 10th 1966, consequent upon consultation with *Kankan Nyame*, Osagyefo's diviner and personal security, Ambrose Yankey told him that they had gazed into the crystal ball and seemed to sense that Ambassador Ebny Whitetones was not as much a friend of Ghana as he professed. As always, Nkrumah immediately believed this oracular pronouncements and went on to cause his withdrawal "because of the suspicion that he may be engaged in activities incompatible with his status."

Washington complied accordingly and also accepted Nkrumah's insistence that the new man should also be a black man. His replacement was a certain Franklin H. Williams, an Afro-American who happened to have been Nkrumah's alumnus at Lincoln University. Whatever the precise nature of *Kankan Nyame*'s or Yankey's divination, it would go down to the credit of Nkrumah's belief in the powers of the supernatural that they smelt a rat however vaguely. But, in point of fact, history would also show that he was shutting the gate when the birds had already flown for, this instinctual action merely goaded the plotters against the regime into quicker action.

The Ghanaian army officers who were to do the damage did not need any further promptings from the American embassy. All was soon set and they now waited with feverish expectations for the day when Nkrumah would be absent from the country, for whatever reason, for the plan to be put into action. Ironically, this anxiety was made all the more easy when Ebny Whitestone was recalled to Washington because, somehow, it would absolve Washington of involvement in the plot.

The American government, and by implication, its ambassadors knew that ever since the 1965 London Commonwealth Prime Ministers' Conference when the decision was made to send a peace mission to Vietnam, Nkrumah had been making preparations to lead such a mission. He was ready to go to Vietnam with peace proposals in July, but the visit was postponed because Ho Chi Minh informed him that for security reasons he could not invite Nkrumah unless the Americans stopped the bombing. Now, with that trip being the only setback to the hatching of the plot, when Nkrumah was encouraged to raise raised the issue of travelling with his fellow alumnus, Ambassador Williams – the latter had given him to believe that Most Americans were fed up with the war and would welcome the intervention of a leader of world status like himself - all omens were in his favour. Whether Williams was aware of the mischief afoot or not will never be fully established but there was no way he could have remained ignorant of it. What is known is that he immediately cabled the State Department. To put final touches on the trip, Nkrumah's Foreign Minister, Quaison Sackey had no difficulty "persuading" President Lyndon B. Johnson to suspend the bombing in Vietnam to allow the peace mission to be effected.

The news that the Hanoi mission would now be undertaken in complete safety fed Nkrumah's ego tremendously. That the world would come to a standstill and the bombs would remain silent for him to go and return in safety was the most eloquent testimony that he, Osagyefo, was a force to reckon with.

***

On the 19th February, two nights before he was to leave for the Hanoi peace talks, Nkrumah was wakened from his sleep by a loud scream from his wife.

"What's the matter, my queen," he asked.

"I found myself being choked to death," she began, trembling like one in the grip of a fever.

"How's that?" Nkrumah asked.

"You left me in bed and went into your study or to the toilet or something like that, and then when I waited for you and you were not coming back I tried to come to you. I found myself surrounded by four windowless walls which began to close in on me as they got smaller and smaller. That's why I cried."

"And what do you make of that?" he asked her.

"I don't know, Osagyefo. Just that I feel shaken."

"Go to sleep," Nkrumah commanded her with a knowing smile. "It's just a dream. Osagyefo tears down all walls. Osagyefo creates windows where there are none."

She shrugged and settled back down to sleep. The following morning she reminded Nkrumah of the dream which she said still hovered in her mind and haunted her with the vividness of a real event. Nkrumah said nothing about it but noted it down as one of the things he would ask Yankey to discuss with *Kankan Nyame* as soon as he returned from Hanoi.

***

As was the tradition whenever Nkrumah was to leave the country for any of his numerous trips abroad, that Tuesday 21st February 1966 was virtually a public holiday in Accra. Since all the civil servants and all Party functionaries, teachers (and school children by implication), and the market women were die-hard members of the CPP, they all lined the streets from the Flag Staff House to the

Accra International Airport, singing party songs, waving party flags. At the airport grounds the women's wing together with the Winneba Ideological Institute choir had filled the air with praise songs to Osagyefo, (victorious in war), *Kantamanto* (one never guilty, one who never goes back on his word), Teacher and Author of the Revolution, *Oeadeeyie* (one who puts things right), Man of Destiny, Star of Africa, Deliverer of Ghana, Iron Boy, the Messiah, His High Dedication. To Kotoka and Afrifa, a familiar member of the women's choir was the famous Auntie Benedicta. She would collapse and die of heart attack on the 25 February when she would hear her own son, Kotoka announcing that he was the leader of the coup d'état that had overthrown Kwame Nkrumah.

After a brief press conference at which Nkrumah told the Ghanaian press that the trip to Hanoi was the crowning stroke of his entire life as a politician as well as a milestone in the exhibition of Black Power, he and his entourage of about sixty persons – including nearly his entire cabinet – climbed into the plane amidst great cheers.

Amongst those who had come to see him off were Kotoka, Afrifa and Harlley, Chief of Police together with his assistant. So far, everything had gone according to plan except for a few hitches. The most disturbing thing was something that should not have bothered Kotoka at all, had he not been inwardly guilty. This was a feeling of uneasiness that came over him as a result of the presence and apparently innocent pronouncements of a certain nuisance.

The man, probably mad or mentally unbalanced, or with some vital screws missing from his makeup, went by several appellations, depending on the part of Accra in which he was at the time - Prophet Shah Mohamet, Malashi, Man-In-charge, MC, Protocol, E.T. Mensah, Professor, Doctor, et al. But his most popular name, and the one he called himself by, was Prophet Shah Mohamet. His true origin was veiled in mystery: he himself claimed that he was a messenger from God who had come down to save Ghana, that from time to time God made revelations to him which he was compelled to reveal to mankind. A certain version claimed that, actually, he was of the Kom tribe of the North West Province of Cameroon. His real name as recorded at the International Students Hostel was Bobe Kuntang Ayah, and that he had come to Ghana in the entourage of a leading freedom fighter and a personal friend of Nkrumah, Dr. Felix Moumié who had fled from attempts to arrest and kill him by President Ahmadou Ahidjo. Felix Moumié, like Nkrumah, staked his entire life fighting against French imperialism and neo-colonialism in Cameroon and as a result, had received much support and encouragement from Nkrumah for his U.P.C. Party (Union des Populations du Cameroun) which was branded in Cameroon as a terrorist organisation and banned. A hunted man all his life, Moumié left Ghana for Europe promising to make arrangements for Bobe Kuntang and his other comrades to join him sometime later.

Unfortunately Moumié's enemies caught up with him in Geneva where he was poisoned in a hotel. That completely destabilised Mohamet who, also among the wanted men in Cameroon was condemned to remain in Ghana. As time went on he tried his hand at several activities: trading, counterfeiting, drug peddling, home tutoring in French, and then a life of petty crimes which eventually landed him in jail for a year or so. It was during this period of abysmal uncertainty and frustration that he began to assume so many different names and identities.

One popular version had it that he was originally from Somalia, that around 1960 he was a student in the Faculty of International Relations at the University of Ghana. The story went that he was among the types of students who believed in enjoying themselves because they were on the United Nations scholarship, that they were paid in foreign currency which they converted in the black market in Lome and became extremely rich, richer even than some of their lecturers. It is said that at a certain examination for which he had not sufficiently prepared he was said to have found that two of the very few questions he had revised the previous night featured amongst the questions given out to them. He was said to have shouted in excitement, the invigilator was said to have called in the campus guards who were said to have whisked him out of the examination room and out of the campus for disturbing the others. As he continued to fight back he was said to have been taken to the university hospital where he was said to have been placed under sedatives. Regaining consciousness he was said to have discovered that he had missed the examinations. Thereafter, madness had set in, reducing him to the public nuisance that he now was.

An unusually gifted individual, he was at home with any of the major Ghanaian languages which he spoke with the flare of a native expert. He was a consummate entertainer who could play the guitar, the flute, the mouth organ, the accordion and the bugle, and dance just a well. Sometimes he did not even need any instruments: he could, by drumming on his belly and striking his bare feet flat on the ground while blowing with his lips, produce very entertaining and rhythmic sounds. He was also a contortionist who could hold a crowd spellbound just by twisting his body and legs round his neck while singing and dancing at the same time.

Despite the fact that he had been to prison, he was no criminal in the serious sense of the word. He was just a simple, harmless, wanderer who took great pleasure in everything that he did to please and entertain. He always hung around where the action was - bars, night clubs, death celebrations, birthday parties, football matches. Quite often, too, he hung around the Officers' Mess at Accra where he would entertain soldiers and ex-servicemen with stories of guerrilla tactics they used to employ in Cameroon to outwit French soldiers.

One key aspect of his entertainment programme was news about promotions and appointments into high positions in government. He would take time to make a list of real life civil servants and then read the offices to which they had been promoted. He would also come up with a list of persons whom Nkrumah planned to dismiss for incompetence. On a few occasions, definitely by sheer coincidence, he had read the names of persons who were appointed soon after that. Another pet subject for entertainment was impending deaths and heinous crimes that had been perpetrated and the high government officials, lawyers and policemen behind the crimes. Generally these were mere fabrications but people enjoyed listening to him while they ate or drank. It was even said that some highly placed persons with an axe to grind fed him with information in order to embarrass their enemies.

Then there was always the impending attempts on Nkrumah's life! He would say, for instance, that Nkrumah would not come out for the next week because the Ewes or the Ashantis had planned to throw a grenade at him. And because he knew that there was some friendship building between the Ewes and the Ashantis which Nkrumah did not like, he would go so far as to name army officers who had been arrested because of a coup they were planning. He would even announce the day and place where the culprits were to be publicly executed. On two occasions after Kotoka, Afrifa and Harlley had hatched their plot, he confronted Kotoka who took such offence that some people became a bit suspicious at his anger.

"It won't work, it won't work, that your plan," he said to Kotoka. "Osagyefo will not go to China. He will remain here and hang you people."

Kotoka informed Harlley about it, but the latter told him to dismiss it from his mind. He also informed Afrifa about it. It was at Afrifa's instigation that Harlley sent his boys to lay hands on the Prophet. Even there in jail he continued to foresee doom and to accuse high-ranking army and police officers. Sadly, after the coup he disappeared into thin air while still in jail. It was believed that he had been murdered by officials who thought his jokes had become too expensive, too unpalatable.

That was the only problem that the conspirators encountered. A week before, Afrifa had come down and the two of them had driven to Takoradi and brought back the parcels in the keeping of Auntie Benedicta. A shadow cabinet had already been formed and a committee set up for the financing of the adventure. The committee knew and was presented with only one of the parcels. Kotoka, Afrifa and Harlley who had long become part of the team of conspirators, decided on where to keep it and on when to bring it out.

***

On that fateful Tuesday morning, as the plane was warming up to leave, Kotoka thought he should give the President a word of caution and encouragement. "Take care of yourself, Osagyefo. There are too many bombs flying over Vietnam."

"Never mind Charley," Nkrumah responded, bubbling with pride, "the bullet that will kill Osagyefo is not yet cast. Even the bombs will stay silent until Osagyefo is back in his Ghana."

There was a very loud applause. Nkrumah then mounted the gangway flanked in front and behind by his entourage of cabinet ministers and other personnel, to the chant of "Osagyefo! Osagyefo!" by the Women's Section of the Party.

The jet began to pick up steam with an ear-splitting crescendo in readiness to wheel to the runway and take off. After the last member of his entourage disappeared into the plane and it looked like any moment the door of the aircraft would be shut in preparation to take off, something very unusual happened which nearly changed the course of the history of Ghana forever. The engine of the plane slowed down and two of the propellers wound to a halt. The staircase was lowered and, to the dismay of everybody, the door of the plane swung open and a few minutes afterwards President Nkrumah re-emerged followed closely behind by Ambrose Yankey, his proverbial clairvoyant and Quaison Sackey and Kwesi Armah and began climbing down. The singing stopped suddenly and everybody looked on in amazement as the men climbed right down. The feelings of the traitors can be more imagined than described when it looked as if Nkrumah had called off the trip.

Nkrumah had always been thought to have superhuman instincts. And, had he really called off the trip he would have saved Africa the shame and embarrassment that his overthrow caused the entire continent. His sudden reappearance outside was a result of a brief conversation that had arisen between him and Yankey as soon as they were informed to tighten their seatbelts in readiness to take off.

"What day is this, my man?" Nkrumah had asked Yankey with visible unease.

The man, suspecting the full implications of the question but, not anxious to lose the first opportunity of his life to visit China and bring back Chinese souvenirs to his expectant loved ones, had replied deviously:

"Tomorrow is Wednesday, Osagyefo. Nothing to fear, Osagyefo. Anything to worry I should know, Osagyefo. "

Nkrumah tried hard to believe in the pronouncement of his oracle but it would not work. In the end he signalled the air hostess in attendance whom he asked to draw the attention of the Captain of the plane. Before the Captain came Nkrumah was already giving instructions to Quaison Sackey to the effect that he should represent him at Hanoi because he was feeling too unwell to undertake the journey. Quaison Sackey was still trying to explain to his President the importance of the mission to the politics of Ghana, Africa and the world, which he said could not be undertaken by a representative of any calibre. Nkrumah had then whispered something in the Captain's ear and then risen with his three lieutenants and they left the plane.

Nkrumah certainly had some violent foreboding, but his vanity took the better of him when he reached the ground. Would he, because of a whim, let slip the one opportunity which was surely going to crown his labours with so much glory? That did not seem likely. That was when he beckoned to Kotoka.

More dead than alive from guilt and fear, and with perspiration sliding down his spine and sides and scalp in rivulets, the officer moved with trembling steps towards his President, his mind frightfully recalling not only the revelations of Prophet Shah Mohamet, but Sections 341 and 342, Part 9 of the Criminal Code – Offences Against the Safety of the State – which every soldier knew by rote.

Section 341 read

"Whoever instigates any foreigner to invade the Gold Coast with armed force shall be liable to suffer death."

Section 342 read:

"Whoever attacks or prepares to attack with armed forces any persons within the Gold Coast, or proceeds or prepares to attack with armed force any person within the Gold Coast, shall be liable to imprisonment for life."

When they sat and hatched the plot with Ebny Whitestone he had no moral compunctions, or apprehensions because they were sworn to secrecy. Now he felt different, very different. He was sure that Nkrumah had discovered through his numerous sources that he had betrayed him. He was sure that Nkrumah was coming to accuse him and immediately order his arrest for high treason.

He would pull his loaded pistol by his side and shoot himself out of the place, rather than submit to be publicly disgraced and executed. He recalled with heartburning self condemnation the suggestion which he had caused the American agent to reject. Members of the inner council of the plotters, particular the police and Ankrah, had suggested that as soon as Nkrumah had finished inspecting the guard of honour at the airport they should open fire on him. He had suggested to the contrary, and in this he was backed by the Americans, that it would be too risky, too blatant. Now he was going to live or die with the consequences of his own decision! What a pity!

While he still stood there turning over these horrible alternatives in his mind, Nkrumah whispered in his ear:

"Keep the throne and the house of your master safe and clean until he returns, you understand?"

Kotoka thought he had not heard him well. But, frozen with fright, with trembling lips and clattering teeth, he managed to say indistinctly:

"You can count on me, Osagyefo,"

"Listen to no imperialist neo-colonialist trash-eh"

"Never, Osagyefo."

With Nkrumah leading the way back, the three men took quick steps up into the plane. It gathered momentum and then took off.

Chapter Ten

As soon as the plane was well in the air, and finally lost in the clouds, the coup plotters went into council to put finishing touches on the very delicate job in hand. They were the four army officers: J.A. Ankrah (who was to be chairman when the dust had settled), Colonel E.K. Kotoka, A. k. Ocran and A.A Afrifa. There were also four police officers: J.W.Harlley, B.A. Yakubu, J.E. Nunoo and A.K. Deku. Undaunted by the near failure of the plot due to Nkrumah's prescience, they worked feverishly into the night.

***

The coup in Ghana began at early in the morning 24 February 1966, when some 600 soldiers of the Kumasi garrison were ordered to move southwards towards Accra. En route, the convoy was stopped by Colonel E.K. Kotoka, Commander of the Second Infantry Brigade Group and Major A.A Afrifa of the Second Brigade. Afrifa took over command of the men while Kotoka went to Accra to report progress to chief of police Harlley. More excited by the opportunity that lay in their path to remain rich forever, neither Kotoka nor Afrifa could recall a word of all the grievances which the American Ambassador had used to convince them to take up arms against Nkrumah.

Now left to their own devices, they knew that with the army and police behind them, anything would work, and that no lie was too blatant to be told. And so, the troops were told that Nkrumah had left Ghana for good, taking with him £8 million, and that as Ghana was without a government it was the duty of the army to assume control to maintain law and order. They added to the ridiculous and preposterous justification the fact that Russian planes were landing at a secret airstrip in northern Ghana and that for days Russian soldiers had been secretly entering Flagstaff House through a tunnel from Accra airport. And then, some element of truth strayed into their thought processes: it had been discovered as part of Nkrumah's intention, so the traitors said, to send Ghanaian troops to fight in Rhodesia where they would face certain death. In addition, his formation of a people's militia threatened the very existence of a professional army. If they wished, therefore, to save both themselves and Ghana, they must seize Flagstaff House.

In the days ahead, they stumbled on more refined means of winning the hearts of the people. It began with the soldiers: as though the violent overthrow of Nkrumah had thrown open the gates of the storerooms of plenty, brand new uniforms were not only promised, but made instantly available. In an effort to deify Nkrumah when the going was good, his sycophantic agents, mainly graduates from the Ideological Institute in Winneba, would visit targeted schools. They would interrupt classes to show the children how greater than God Nkrumah was! They would ask the children to pray to God to give them biscuits and cookies and sweets. The poor children would pray and weep, but to no avail. The brainwashers would then ask them to ask the almighty Osagyefo to answer to their needs. Even before they finished asking, sweets and biscuits and cookies would be rained on them through the windows.

Now, the soldiers followed the same route, but reversed the order: it was just enough to curse and disown Nkrumah and every other thing would be added unto them. People who defamed him publicly, especially on television, were given lucrative appointments in the new dispensation. This was not exactly what the CIA would have recommended, but for the coup plotters, whatever worked the best was the best. Nothing was considered too absurd or ridiculous if it helped keep them in power.

***

In her very informative book – KWAME NKRUMAH: A BIOGRAPHY - June Milne has carefully documented events that took place, although it is done from a pro-Nkrumah perspective:

In the early morning of 24 February, Brigadier Hassan, the Head of Military Intelligence was arrested. But Colonel Zanerigu, the Commander of the Presidential Guard Regiment escaped arrest and was able to drive to Flagstaff House to warn the garrison. Major-General Barwah, Deputy Chief of Defence Staff, who was in command of the army while the Chief of Defence Staff, General Aferi, was abroad, was woken from his sleep by the arrival at his house of Kotoka and some twenty-soldiers. He was invited to join the traitors; when he refused he was shot dead in front of his wife and children. In the meantime, Harlley had arranged for the arrest of most of Nkrumah's ministers and leading CPP officials. By 6 a.m., with the help of troops under the command of A.K. Ocran, the airport, cable office and radio station had been seized. Kotoka broadcast that the army and police had taken over the government of Ghana. But fighting was still going on at Flagstaff House where Presidential Guard Regiment resisted fiercely. This continued for several hours, until Kotoka was able to order from the combined Army/Police HQ which he had set up at Police Headquarters, the intervention of the Second Battalion. However, the defenders of Flagstaff House, although fighting against overwhelming odds, refused to surrender until the rebels threatened to blow up the house in which Nkrumah's elderly mother and his wife and three young children lived. Rebel troops ransacked Flagstaff House,' smashing windows and furniture, ripping telephones from desks, and destroying anything they could lay their hands on. Nkrumah's own office was singled out for special treatment, and the large collection of books and manuscripts which he kept there was destroyed. Madam Fathia, Nkrumah's Egyptian-born wife, had fled with her three children to the Egyptian Embassy, and a few days later they were put on a flight for Cairo. His (Nkrumah's)mother was told to go 'where you belong' and was taken by some friends to the village of Nkroful where Nkrumah was born.

Fathia, Nkrumah's wife narrated the traumatic events of that fateful morning to inquisitive journalists at the Cairo International Airport on her arrival there:

"It was the lions who first made me suspect that there was something amiss," she said.

"Lions?" a journalist enquired.

"Yes lions," she replied. "Near where we lived there were caged lions. People used to come there and admire them. My little son, Gamel and his younger brother, Sekou woke me up to say that the lions were crying as if they were out of the cage. We were truly frightened. It was only later that we learned that in the confusion that followed the army take over they forgot to feed the lions. An then, while we were still wondering what could make the lions roar so angrily, we heard gunshots in the direction of the airport. Then suddenly the radio was turned on and then I heard the broadcast by Colonel Kotoka, announcing the coup. I took fright."

"How did the children react to the news? How did you explain it to them?" another journalist asked.

"They did not know what it all meant. But I just told them that we must try to get to the Egyptian embassy and that the soldiers had taken over the country from their dad. They still did not quite understand what I meant. And when I repeated that we must leave they went into their rooms and were carefully parking their things. They thought it was a kind of pleasure trip we were about to undertake. Poor things!"

"Did you immediately leave for the embassy?"

"I phoned the embassy and asked them to call my father, President Nasser and tell him what trouble we were in. As God would have it, as soon as I finished talking the telephone lines went dead because they had cut them."

"So you couldn't get a reply from the embassy?"

"I couldn't and decided not to wait for one. I took my three children and started out for the embassy."

"And the luggage, what did you take along?"

"Nothing, just our lives. I told the children to leave everything behind. I took a suitcase, that's all."

"And on your way, did they recognize you?"

"They did,"

"They did not molest you?"

"That's why I say Allah is great. only just managed to reach the nearby Egyptian embassy. The embassy had been informed that there was an Egyptian plane at the airport bound for Cairo. So we just left the embassy for the airport. Between the embassy and the airport our car was stopped by tanks and troops at an army roadblock. I and the children were ordered out of the car at gunpoint. The officer in charge looked at me with great surprise, as if seeing me for the first time. I saw him report by radio and ask for instructions as to what to do with us. Eventually, we were allowed to proceed to the airport to board the Egyptian aircraft."

"Have you been able to contact President Nkrumah?"

"I haven't and I don't even know where to do so. I think my father will be able to do that for us."

Chapter Eleven

Nkrumah travelled by Ghana Airways – a DC10 - from Accra to Rangoon in Burma. The Chinese government had sent a plane to take him from Burma to China. At the airport in Peking he was welcomed by Prime Minister Chou-En-Lai and Liu Shao-Chi, together with other officials including the Chinese Ambassador in Accra who had gone on ahead to Peking to be there to meet him.

Everybody on the airport grounds had heard about the coup d'état in Ghana and

they had combined and cancelled ideas as to how the news would be broken to their august guest. So nervous were they all that there was nobody bold enough to talk to Nkrumah verbally about it. In the end it had been agreed that the heartbreaking news be written on a piece of paper which they attached on a conspicuous spot on the bouquet of flowers that was to be presented to him as soon as he descended from the plane.

There was high drama as Nkrumah received the bouquet of flowers beaming with

a smile but, suspecting nothing, did not even look at the bunch of white lilies, roses and clovers which the Chinese Ambassador's niece had been instructed to present to him. He simply kissed the little girl on both cheeks and then transferred the bouquet to the closest member of his entourage, his Foreign Minister, Quaison Sackey. As Nkrumah proceeded with the ceremonial handshake, the Chinese Ambassador from Accra withdrew from the line of worried personalities and tried to signal the Foreign Minister to read the note attached to the flowers.

Quaison Sackey was a stranger to sign language and so, not quite understanding what he was being called upon to do, the Minister instead handed the bouquet to the person next to him, Kwesi Armah, Minister of Trade. Quaison was a very smart individual and so as he looked again at the Chinese Ambassador, he concluded that there was something the man was trying to communicate to him. He walked across to meet the Chinese Premier and put his ear near the Chinese Ambassador's mouth. The man whispered into Quaison's ear. The Minister withdrew and stared into the Ambassador's face with alarming disbelief. The Ambassador nodded to confirm what he was saying. Quaison Sackey immediately returned to join his compatriots. He then took back the bouquet of flowers and read the note before nervously showing it round to his colleagues, perspiration bursting instantly in the face of everybody who read it. Within a few minutes they had all read it.

Meanwhile, and as he usually did in foreign company, Nkrumah was at his ebullient best: he praised the Chinese Ambassador's charcoal grey suit, praised the Chinese Premier's warm handclasp, and nodded at the Chinese art and architecture.

"I envy you over here," he said to the Chinese premier. "When a people are left to express themselves unhindered," he went on, "the sky is the limit. We are trying something like this in Kumasi university back home. But for the brainwashing of imperialist colonialists…"

Unaware of the tension in the air he continued to chat with his hosts as they moved towards the airport lounge and then drove immediately to the Guest House where Nkrumah was to stay. "This weather is wonderful," he remarked.

"Ya, spring is setting in," the Chinese Premier said.

Nkrumah sank into the large cushion chair and breathed a sigh of relief. Then he threw his head backwards until it touched the backrest of the comfortable chair that was shown to him, and tried to take a well-deserved rest after a long and exhausting flight. The key members of his Sixty-six member entourage – mainly the Ministers and Secretaries of State - ringed him on both sides. He was just about to close his eyes when the Chinese Prime Minister thought he could withhold the news no longer.

"Mr. President," he sat up and said, leaning towards Nkrumah, "I have some bad

news for you."

Nkrumah opened his eyes with a start and stared in the direction of the speaker

but without saying anything.

"There is a coup d'état back in your country, Ghana."

"There is a what?"

"A coup d'état."

"In Guinea or Ghana?"

"Ghana," everybody said including members of his entourage.

"You have been overthrown by a military coupin Ghana. The Army and the Police have taken over control of the country."

Nkrumah turned round to look into the faces of his men. His eyes met those of Ambrose Yankey who had made it a habit of always standing or sitting close to him. It was a very brief stare but Yankey received it like a wounding arrow. In it he read: "You were supposed to protect me. What were you doing that you didn't see this coming?"

"I have been betrayed," he cried, shaking his head. "I have been betrayed. Osagyefo has been betrayed. Harold Wilson and Lyndon Johnson have finally had their way. They finally did it. They have finally shattered a dream that was too big for them to bear, those imperialist, neo-colonialist bastards," he vituperated.

The ghost of a smile then crossed his deflated visage. A tired smile. A smile which did not certainly come from his heart for [one is reminded here of the Chelsea cat in Lewis

Carroll's *Alice in Wonderland* which disappeared leaving behind its smile], the smile belied the acrimony with which he spoke of Britain and America. His visage underwent an instant transfiguration. Almost immediately his jaws sank and two deep gorges of age marks appeared on each side of his face like a pair of magical dividers. Suddenly his pronounced forehead with its receding hair, rose in contours of worry lines.

Although at that time it sounded like a wild guess from the lips of somebody whose considered opinion of the imperialists was one of unmitigated condemnation, it did not take too long for the world to establish that the USA Central Intelligence Agency (CIA) was involved in planning the coup. In a very well documented work some ten years afterwards - *In Search of Enemies* - William Stockwell admitted that the CIA station in Accra' was given a generous budget and maintained intimate contact with the plotters as a coup was hatched.... Inside CIA headquarters, the Accra station was given full, if unofficial credit for the eventual coup.' The CIA station chief in Accra, Howard T. Bane, was rewarded with promotion to a senior position in the Agency. Nkrumah, certainly, was in no doubt about foreign involvement. In a message sent to Sékou Touré on 25 February 1966, the day after the coup, Nkrumah wrote:

'This incident in Ghana is a plot by the imperialists, neo-colonialists and their agents in Africa.... We must strengthen our resolution and fight for the dignity of our people to the last man, and for the unity of Africa.'

He was convinced the embassies of the USA, Britain and West Germany were all implicated in the plot to overthrow the CPP government. He considered that the Afro-American US ambassador in Accra at that time, Franklin Williams, was closely involved. For it would have been extremely unlikely he did not know what was going on in the embassy with CIA officers operating from there.

Nkrumah's vehement and ceaseless accusations, however biased and blatant, had one small advantage in working against the coup plotters. The night that the coup plot was hatched, the traitors, knowing their own limitations as soldiers not exposed to any deep knowledge of statecraft, had expressed fears of the American sponsors abandoning them in the thick of things, in the middle of the river, as they put it. The American Ambassador had reassured them that his government would remain with them and guide and assist them all the way. Because of the loud accusations being levelled against them, the Americans or any other western power could not offer any help to Ghana without drawing suspicion and accusations on itself. As a result, when the NLC needed technological assistance or advice on what to do all they got came in the nature of media hype about the "bloodlessness" and "popularity of the coup."

This apparently insignificant detail explains, although it does not justify, why the coup brought Ghana down to its knees, and it would take so many decades, so many other coups, so many executions of heads of state and so much suffering, for her to get back on the winning track. The fate of Ghana, however, was of no consequence to the neo-colonialists. Their principal aim had been achieved – Kwame Nkrumah, that thorn in their flesh, had been removed.

***

At the announcement and confirmation of the military take over the Prime Minister whose eyes were pinned on Nkrumah's every movement, noticed how the latter tightened his lips and nodded as if telling himself: "I knew it, I could see it coming."

There was dead silence across the room.

"If this is a joke," Nkrumah said looking at the Prime Minister and the other dignitaries who had come to receive him "it is in very bad taste. I must return to Ghana forthwith.

I must talk to my people. Osagyefo cannot, repeat, cannot be overthrown. Quaison, Kwesi, Bossman," he turned to his henchmen. "Get the plane ready."

"Plane, Osagyefo?"

"The DC10…"

"It left us to return to Ghana since Rangoon, Osagyefo."

"Mr. Prime Minister," he said in a state of mind dithering on a nervous

breakdown. "I won't proceed to Hanoi. Everybody must understand."

"I understand, Mr. President. I understand. We all do understand."

"Mr. Prime Minister, give me a plane. Place a plane at my disposal. Osagyefo

cannot be a *former* president even for one minute."

"Just cool your mind, Mr. President," the Prime Minister said. "Everything will be made available to you. Just rest your mind a little."

Nkrumah tried to close his eyes but finding that he could not pretend, he sat up and signalled to the Chinese Ambassador to come and sit by him. The old man, seeing that Nkrumah needed more consoling, walked across to the fallen president with whom he had had such a very good working relationship and stood listening from a standing position with his hands clasping and unclasping nervously behind him.

"But word reaching us has confirmed that your family is safe. Your wife and kids have arrived Cairo in one piece," the old man added. This last bit of information was calculated, the man must have thought, to mitigate the effect on Nkrumah and make the loss a lot more bearable. Most human beings upon receipt of such mind-shattering news would ask: "Any news about my family? Did they do any harm to either my wife or my children?" And if the answer is "No," they would take a deep breath and say something like "Thank God for that at least."

Nkrumah's reaction to that detail took the Chinese Prime Minister completely by surprise. He did not know that Nkrumah would even have been glad to hear that she had been hurt, because that would have inflamed President Nasser to take his revenge on the traitors.

Chapter Twelve

At this point it is necessary to mention Nkrumah's ambivalent attitude towards women as well as the family. Like most women of Oriental stock, Fathia Rizk was a woman of great charm. When she arrived Ghana she reminded many Ghanaians of the breathtakingly beautiful ladies that featured in Indian films that were enormously popular in Ghana at the time. Guests to the Nkrumah household described her as a very caring hostess, a devoted mother as well as a very accommodating housewife.

But it was not for any of these virtues that Nkrumah had married her, and Nkrumah could just as well have married her even if she were a caricature or a cripple. At the time he asked for her hand, he had carefully worked out how squarely such a relationship would fit into the frame of things, as far as the realization of his wider political ambitions went.

In his pan-African vision, the Arabic-speaking states of North Africa of which Egypt was the most influential or was capable of wielding a lot of influence, were no less African than those predominantly non-Arab states south of the Sahara. As the most vociferous proponent of pan-Africanism Nkrumah guessed rightly that a conjugal union with an Egyptian national was likely to win the minds of Egyptians to his side like nothing else. It was the surest means of strengthening his much-cherished Arab-African ties.

The scheming Nkrumah went even further than just marriage: he named his son Gamel after Gamal Abdel Nasser, an act which endeared him all the more to the

Egyptian leader. And until his death (and even long afterwards), a bond of everlasting friendship existed between Nasser (and the Arabs by implication) and himself. Over and above the fact that Nasser was the President of Egypt, he was a strong advocate of the African component of the Egyptian national composition, the first Egyptian leader to do so.

His relationship with his wife must be understood only in that light. This can be amply illustrated from the will he drew up on 18th February just before he left Ghana on that fateful trip. In it, we see how clearly he subordinated family ties to his political commitments. Paragraph 2 reads:

I Direct further that the Executors herein so appointed shall until the duration of this testament remain irrevocably Executors and Trustees of this my will and shall so ensure that this Will is firmly and truly administered and they shall be given and entitled to every assistance and access to my properties in the due performance of their trust. Now therefore I Bequeath all my earthly belongings of whatsoever kind and whosesoever situated free of legacy duty (if any) and all other (if any) duty payable upon or by reason of my death to the convention people's party and

I Direct that the said Convention People's Party shall under take to maintain, provide for, educate and to do all things in such a manner as to ensure that proper upkeep, livelihood and maintenance of my mother, my wife and children including any adopted child or children; should any legatees who survive me required to be under guardianship, tuition, protection, domestic assistance and / or help shall so set aside such sums as shall be sufficient to provide for them and any other contingencies as would enable them to live in a manner worthy of my name.

So long as the welfare of the CPP was taken care of, he did not particularly care about his wife and children. This was very unusual but, as far as Nkrumah was concerned, quite natural. And since his overthrow, he never cared to see either his wife or the children until his death. His seemingly casual and even absurd attitude towards his wife and family can hardly be interpreted as a lack of knowledge of how great a political weapon women can become if properly rallied. Nkrumah would have been the first to admit that they formed a bulwark of his party. In a rather biased account of the life of Kwame Nkrumah, Peter Omari has affirmed that:

Nkrumah's low opinion of human nature seemed to find an exception in his attitude towards women. He used to say that all his life he had been successful with women, whom he found loyal and devoted. Whenever he entrusted any task to a woman, he was sure it would be executed with zeal and devotion. But although Nkrumah demanded absolute loyalty and fanatical devotion from his aides, he himself did not seem to regard them as more than instruments to be used and then discarded when no longer useful.

Be it as it may, Nkrumah could very rightly be counted amongst the very first African leaders to advocate gender equality. A major aspect of the CPP policy was the enhancement of the political and civic rights of women. Nkrumah catapulted women onto the political scene in a way that was new both in Ghana and Africa. For him, this was part of the attempt at projecting the African Personality and at raising the status of African womanhood. In this light, therefore, provision was made for the election of women to the National Assembly. Ten Women parliamentarians took their seats at the first session of the First Republic of Ghana in 1961.

Women were appointed to serve on boards of corporations, schools and town councils. A few women served on the Central Committee of the CPP. Increasing numbers of women entered courses of higher education, many pursuing training courses abroad qualifying them to occupy most of the positions previously held exclusively by men. In addition, discriminatory provisions relating to women's work were abolished, and equal pay instituted for equal work. Maternity leave on full pay was assured. Women underwent pilot training in the Ghana Air Force Training School at Takoradi. Women were encouraged to enrol in the army to train alongside men in the infantry, in the intelligence and service corps, and to become electrical and mechanical engineers.

Among the most enthusiastic supporters of the CPP were the market women, always a very strong voice in the country. Not only did they contribute generously to party funds, but together with local government councils they controlled much of the trading life of their communities. Nkrumah had the greatest respect for them, ever mindful of their power and good sense. Demonstrations of market women would be quickly organized on occasions when it was deemed necessary, or when their interests were perceived to be threatened.

The National Council of Ghana Women (NCGW) was inaugurated by Nkrumah on 10 September 1960 as an integral wing of the CPP. The NCGW, with branches throughout the country, was to be the only recognized women's organization, and to be represented on the party's Central Committee. With the formation of the NCGW the Women's Section of the party ceased to exist. Members of the Council frequently formed part of Nkrumah's entourage on his travels overseas when they studied the position of women and their organizations abroad.

Two months before the inauguration of the NCGW, the Conference of Women of Africa and of African descent was held in Accra. In his opening address, Nkrumah spoke of the mission the women of Africa had to fulfil in working actively with men in liberating and unifying the continent, and projecting the African Personality. At the time of the Ghana-Guinea-Mali Union, a Council of Women of the Union of African States was formed. At the second conference in Accra, Nkrumah called attention to the sufferings the people of the Congo, Angola, Mozambique, South Africa and Namibia, urging Africa's need for 'a new woman,' dedicated and inspired by the high ideals of patriotism and African unity.

Kwame Nkrumah was gifted with an unparalleled memory power. And at no time was this gift more evident than when he was recounting his numerous achievements. He was very different from many African leaders, absentee leaders, who were leaders all but in name, who could hardly name any developmental projects in their countries mainly because they were generally away in Europe enjoying themselves while their ministers did their best or their worst. As the cliché went, Nkrumah had his hand in every pie. Thus when the Chinese Prime Minister divulged the news of his overthrow his mind went back to his earliest achievements for Ghana. As if reading from some internal or invisible memoranda, he broke in:

"By 1963, just a few years ago, the per capita national income of my Ghana was the highest in Africa outside South Africa. If you doubt me read the Escott Reid's report in *THE FUTURE OF THE WORLD BANK*. That should give you an idea of why I think there is madness somewhere in Ghana. This was very untypical of that stereotype of an underdeveloped economy as the Imperialist, Neo-colonialists have made a song of saying.

"Look at that report. If the figure of £81 pounds in that year doesn't mean anything to you, just look at comparative figures from the rest of the world around us: Malawi showed £13, Ethiopia, £17; Nigeria £34; UAR £49, and India £32. Furthermore, if my statistics do not now fail me, and they have never failed me," he shouted stamping his fist on the low table in front of him. "The gross domestic product of my Ghana showed an enviably high rate of growth, amounting to 40% in total in the period 1955-1962. This was an average compound annual real rate of growth of 4.8%. This is really high even by the standards of the so-called developed countries. And they say Osagyefo should hand over the stewardship of his Ghana to Imperialists Neo-colonialists bandits and vampires."

The very supportive old man rose to Nkrumah's side and, placing his right hand on Nkrumah's trembling shoulders tried to encourage him further. "In politics, my dear, there are bound to be setbacks. The challenge is never to fall, but to rise with a determination to scale even greater heights. This your coup in Ghana is nothing but a temporary setback. You are still a young man, a very very young man. Other things being equal you should still have at least forty years ahead of you to correct the errors of the past."

Nkrumah looked at the old man with an admixture of disbelief and outrage.

Chapter Thirteen

Nkrumah was by nature a rather light eater. His breakfast generally consisted of grapefruit and perhaps a little cereal and honey, or occasionally an egg and he would work through till 3 pm with only a fruit to sustain him or a cup of herbal tea. His main meal came at about 3 pm. It was a simple two-course meal of meat or fish, followed always by fruit salad. His favourite food was the traditional Ghanaian stew and *fou fou*. The evening meal was little more than a snack.

His doctors often referred to it as jetlag, the airhostesses called it air-sickness, but Nkrumah usually felt a lot of discomfort during and at the end of long flights. On this particular flight, after Rangoon, he had taken a sandwich overlaid with guava jam. And while he had found it difficult to sleep he had succeeded in making substantial modifications to his speech to be delivered at the conference at Hanoi. He had also succeeded in coming up with broad outlines of what he expected his representative to present at the OAU Council of Ministers meeting in Addis Ababa.

The mind-shattering news of his overthrow converted the jetlag into physical pain at the pit of his stomach and he did not feel like eating anything. Thus while his kinsmen had lunch, a doctor whom the Chinese Prime Minister had called in took care of their august visitor. After some pills and few tablets which calmed his nerves he was able to sit up and converse without writhing his body or manifesting any major discomfort. As part of his itinerary, a banquet had long before his arrival been scheduled to take place on his behalf at the Civic Reception Centre in downtown Peking. At 8 pm he and his entourage were to be conducted to the place.

For the banquet and any other major engagements during the Hanoi mission he had made it clear to the important members of his entourage that wherever they would go they would make it a point to leave Ghana's indelible imprint on the minds of their host. They would all be dressed in their *Kente* – heavy homespun traditional loincloth wrapped round the waist and over the right shoulder, over a sparkling white T-shirt. They would also wear the broad home-made Ghanaian slippers to go with the outfit.

Thus, when at 8 pm Quaison Sackey checked on him to get any further instructions on the impending banquet, he came already dressed as the President had instructed them while still in Ghana. To his surprise, he found Nkrumah rather informally dressed. For a while he thought the President had forgotten about the invitation to the banquet. He was wearing a black leather shoe and a long-sleeve black coat-like shirt and a pair of trousers to match. The *Kente*, lay on the floor near the shutter of his large wardrobe, as yet unopened from the package as the valet had packed it. Thinking that the President may not have been aware of how close to the hour of the banquet they were he reminded him politely:

"Any time Osagyefo is ready I would let my people know and we leave. They are all dressed."

"Any time they are ready we go," Nkrumah said without emotion. "What else do we need to do?"

"We forget about our traditional wear, Osagyefo?"

"We forget," Nkrumah responded with a contemptuous twist of the lips.

Quaison was taken aback but he did his best not to show his surprise at this sudden change of heart on the part of the President. It was only then that it began to dawn on him that the news from Ghana hurt him badly. To be sure, Nkrumah never took 'no' for an answer. He was an eternal optimist. It was now becoming clear that his supposed optimism was founded on the belief that he was invulnerable, rather than that he was a shock absorber. He had deluded himself into believing that he was above human destruction, untouchable. His true mettle as just another mortal was beginning to make itself visible.

Although many of his followers stood firmly behind him and his CPP, many of them did so simply because of financial and other benefits accruing there from. Apparently, because of this mercenary attitude towards the Party not one of them was really capable of knowing that the authenticity of Nkrumah's life as indissolubly bound up to his relationship with Ghana. In particular, this had to do with his being the President of Ghana, and he could not by any stretch of the imagination play second fiddle.

The fall from that lofty height as Ghana's number one citizen and foremost African leader down to a contemptible *nothingness* was truly agonizing, a reality so grim that he could hardly imagine how to confront. Suddenly, everything typically Ghanaian repulsed and nauseated him with all its suggestiveness of treachery. And there was much more in store for him! Since receiving the news he was aware by the minute, of a chasm, a void within him that exhausted him of all natural feeling. He felt drained.

The foreign Minister did not press to know why the President had decided to discard the traditional outfit. Not anxious to look more Ghanaian than his President he went back to his people and asked them to change from their Ghanaian attire to other dresses that they considered presentable.

"That's Osagyefo's decision," he added with an disguised tone of finality. . Within a few minutes the persons involved were ready except for the two ladies who were left behind and they finally missed the invitation because it took them a long time to get dressed differently. And the rest of the group could not afford to keep the President waiting on them, even for one minute.

***

Kwame Nkrumah was a man of many parts, a master of body language and an engaging orator to whom every occasion for a public address was a performance and that was very impressive to listen to and very entertaining to watch. As an orator possessing a fiery eloquence, he would bring all his theatrical skills into play when he addressed the public; he was a born actor, who played on the emotions of his audience. For effect, he would use his hands while speaking; he would shake his head, pace along the dais and give a captivating smile., although he tends to curb himself when speaking in the Assembly. He would stroll across the stage, striking his left palm with his right clenched fist to emphasize a point or, returning to the microphone, stamp his fist on the dais to give his every word the strongest emphasis. As a politician he was shrewd, his timing was perfect, and his touch sure. He had a rare gift for perception and assimilation, and a good memory. Among the crowds he could speak straight to their thoughts and feelings. So they felt he was their man. All this because he was always intensely passionate about everything he said, and most of what he said had to do with the greatness of Ghana, set against the threat of colonialism and imperialism.

But he was no longer the same person, try as he could. He had drunk a fruit juice and eaten not at all. But, against all predictions, and with every muscle and every nerve on his body militating against composure, he was able to deliver a rousing speech which drew loud applauses from various corners of the hall.

In all fairness to the audience, however, it must be said that the speech lacked much of his virtuoso performance. That he was not at his best was obvious to the more discerning members of the audience. He was at his worst. He did not stray away from the microphone, did not touch the bottle of mineral water set beside him, and did not reach for his handkerchief which would have been wet from mopping the perspiration that would have been streaming down his forehead. This prompted the keen and observant Chinese Ambassador from Accra who was used to watching Nkrumah speak to remark to Minister Quaison Sackey:

"This news from Ghana has taken something out of the President." To which the man responded:

"Very very much."

"It's such a shame," the Ambassador went on, "it is very rare to find such a leader whose destiny is so tied to that of his country." And the Ambassador meant every word of what he was saying because he, as well as many other Ghanaians and persons who had followed the history of Ghana very closely were well aware that Nkrumah viewed Ghana as his self-acquired personal property, a view that was propagated by his followers. For example, his birthday had been declared as public holiday, to be observed as National Founder's Day. Many people, especially in the other newly independent countries of Africa who were unfamiliar with the progress Ghana had already made before independence believed very strongly that he alone had built modern Ghana.

The loud applauses that filled the air were less from the contents of his delivery than the appreciation of the fact that he was able to muster courage and talk intelligently on other matters while his house was on fire. In particular, he spoke at length on the subject of Afro-Asian solidarity, condemning US policy in Vietnam in vehement terms and calling for the complete withdrawal of their forces so that peace negotiations could begin. However, many amongst the audience who were used to hearing him talk in public were of the opinion that some sting had gone out of his words, and that he was rather tentative at points where in the past he would have been forthrightly and fearlessly bold.

Chapter Fourteen

After the banquet he was persuaded to grant a very brief TV interview which was later said to have been aired in various parts of the world, perhaps and ironically, with the exception of Ghana. In that interview he urged Ghanaians to remain calm, in spite of all the provocation, and promised them that he would set everything back in order as soon as he returned in 48 hours. He ended up by ordering the soldiers to return to the barracks where they belonged. He then retired to his Presidential Suite at the Guest Lodge.

Back and alone in his room, Nkrumah watched with great anguish and listened with unwilling ears, the images on TV and the news over the radio. He could not withstand the sight of the pictures that the Western media kept flashing every thirty minutes on events in Ghana: so-called *jubilant crowds* waving palm fronds and holding high in the air enlarged pictures of the coup plotters. But by far the most disturbing image was that of his fallen statue which lay in broken chunks at the base. Some soldiers could be seen posing for photographs with the butts of their guns resting on the truncated torso. About a few metres from the main body of the statue lay the dismembered right arm that in the statue's erect position pointed to the sky in front in the motion of the familiar CPP motto: "Forward Ever..." The hand, now detached at the elbow, lay buried in debris. Over the radio, the news in the air was just as disheartening for the beleaguered President. All the major radio stations – VOA, Radio Deutschweller, Radio France Intern, the BBC

– which Nkrumah had long branded as mouthpieces of the neo-colonialists/imperialists blood suckers were having a field day, dishing out *ad nauseam* minute by minute of what Nkrumah dismissed as distorted and exaggerated accounts of happenings in Ghana.

Like the proverbial ostrich burying its head in the sand in a desperate bid to hide, Nkrumah sighed and turned both the TV and the radio off. All the radios later declared the coup as a complete and bloodless success in which most of Nkrumah's supporters confessing that they had been either coerced or grossly misled by Nkrumah's magnetism, had declared for the new regime – the NLC. Nkrumah continued to curse the whole world and went under his blanket, bemoaning his fate which now seemed to hang on a very delicate balance. He wished that by shutting his own radio set and turning off his own TV, all radio sets and TVs across the world could be switched off, or that he would wake up to find the whole thing a mere dream.

But that was not to be. Nkrumah was such a high profile personality and Ghana so much in the limelight that anything that happened either to him or to Ghana was instantly considered newsworthy. And this was not just any kind of news! The overthrow of Nkrumah was a news item of such monumental proportion for Africa and the world that journalists everywhere must have something to write home about. While the Chinese press did its best to spread the bad news in all its ramifications, and without restraint, the excitement amongst members of Nkrumah's entourage was indescribable, uninhibited, and downright disconcerting for the President.

From the moment they touched down at Peking International airport, concerned friends, relatives and even authorities in the NLC (National Liberation Council) - the new name for the coup plotters – had been burning telephone lines, cablegram's and every available source of communication, in a bid to reach their loved ones in the Nkrumah entourage to Hanoi. Most of the messages were identical: diplomats, ministers and government workers of high standing in the service of Nkrumah at the so-called Hanoi peace mission were called upon declare their support for the new regime within 48 hours and be pardoned and/ or re-commissioned to new duties or be damned with him. Diplomats in his entourage who support the new regime were being requested to report to the NLC head office in Burma Camp, Accra for briefing and authentication before returning to the erstwhile positions, within that stipulated period.

***

At about 10 pm when the influx of these phone calls and cable messages was at its peak, it occurred to Quaison Sackey, Nkrumah's Minister of Foreign Affairs and the acknowledged leader of the team after Nkrumah to get his people together to gauge the extent to which affairs in Ghana were affecting them and perhaps come up with a consensus or a road map for their future. The invitation was limited only to the Big Six – Quaison himself, Kwesi Armah (Minister of Trade), M.F. Dei-Anang (Ambassador Extraordinary in charge of the African Affairs Secretariat), J.E. Bossman (Ambassador to the UK) F. Arkhurst (Ghana's Permanent Representative at the United Nations), and Ambrose Yankey (President's Chief of Personal Security). Also co-opted were the only two ladies – Mrs. Amankwa Ophelia Oseih and Lady Mensah Ablavi Victoria – representatives of the National Council of Ghana Women (NCGW) on the peace mission.

It has often been said that a guilty mind needs no accuser. When word first went round that Quaison wanted to meet the key members of the entourage, there was general unease.

Everybody knew how close the Minister was to Nkrumah and feared the worst. Everybody knew that Osagyefo had the supernatural powers to smell treachery and so there was the general fear that he might have got wind that defections had been planned and may have arranged for the quislings to be apprehended at once. Their fears were not baseless because, perhaps with the singular exception of Ambrose Yankey, there was not one of them who came for the meeting who had not been contacted more than twice from Ghana, and there was not a single one of them who had already made a commitment of some sort to the changed order of things. The pressure building up within them as a result of the crisis back home and the pledges they were separately being called upon to make had risen to breaking point. Yet, there were no two persons who had shared the secret of the responses made back home.

Again the odd man out was Ambrose Yankey, and for obvious reasons. Although he occupied a very crucial office in Nkrumah's government, everybody knew him to be a man of straw. The transition from fish monger at Takoradi market to head of President's personal security was not easy to take. A second reason for slighting him was the fact that everybody knew that it was because of his self-proclaimed clairvoyant powers that Nkrumah kept him around him. The fact that he could not use his supernatural powers to foresee the doom that awaited Nkrumah and himself on the Hanoi trip ruled him out as a charlatan, a false prophet. Yet, because Quaison suspected that having failed to save Nkrumah he could not be trusted because he might want to make amends by betraying them, he was not invited to the meeting. However, the fears of the people were very quickly dispelled when they now saw that what Quaison called them for was a lot more gladdening than they had all anticipated.

He went straight to the point: the crisis in Ghana.

"I have thought it wise for us to come together and brainstorm on our past, present and future in the light of the upheavals back home. We have all heard separately about what is happening at home at this hour that we are far out here. Let me just brief you about what I have heard:

"There is much brutality and suffering in Accra as troops and police are rounding up hundreds of key CPP personnel and flinging them into prison. Practically the entire CPP leadership throughout the country has already been arrested or that will happen in the days to come. I am talking about all cabinet ministers, members of Parliament, officials of the CPP and all its subsidiary and associate organizations, including trade union leaders. In the course of the operation, many people are being beaten up and their houses looted. Among them are my personal friends, Professor W.E. Abraham, Acting Vice-Chancellor of the University of Ghana, who was beaten unconscious and then flung into a police van; and N.A. Welbeck, Minister of Education and Party Propaganda who had several teeth knocked out and is not sure to survive another week. Attorney-General Geoffrey Bing was also arrested and tortured and has been led to prison." Here he shook his head sadly and there sighs of despondency across the room. He then continued:

"We are far from home, very very far from home I am afraid and unless we proceed with caution, the same fate awaits us, meaning that some of us may never be united with their families and loved ones again. That's food for thought."

He drew in a very deep breath, looked round the room and could notice the dismal mood that enfolded them all. There were no exchange of glances, no under-the-table talks.

Everybody seemed engaged in some kind of soul-searching reflection.

"I want to presume, as I began, that many amongst us have been contacted by highly placed personalities from back home. And we have been called upon to make very hard choices. As they say, to choose between the devil and the deep blue sea. I have responded. I have responded according to the dictates of my conscience, considering the welfare of my family. I have responded according to the dictates of my profession.

"I am not going to tell you what my response has been because I do not want to influence anybody's decision if he or she was still fence-sitting. But if you care, let me add that I am the Minister of Foreign Affairs for my country. Not, repeat NOT, the Minister of Foreign Affairs for an individual."

He stopped talking and it looked like he had stopped not because he had come to the end of his speech but because he sensed that tears were threatening to cloud his eyes.

After sometime he resumed: "Make your choices, but be ready to live with the consequences of your decision. Nobody will die in another's place."

Again, the silence in the room deepened. His position as well as that of many others, vis-à-vis the crisis, was clear: he would declare for the new regime.

Finally Kwesi Armah took the floor. He was a rather tall gentleman of athletic stature. His hair was already greying fast, although he was just about Nkrumah's age. Very fastidious in taste, he always dressed very well, be it in European of African outfit. He was enormously popular amongst the CPP functionaries not just because of his sense of humour, but because he always insisted on prompt action in whatever he was involved. He was also known to be very honest, which was more than could be said about any other senior member of the party. He too was forthright in his approach:

"I personally thank the honourable minister for taking this initiative. If it has achieved anything, it has at least brought us together at this most trying moment when our future and our lives hangs in the balance. Minister Quaison has spoken well in saying he is the Minister for Ghana, not for an individual. Without belabouring the point, let me declare here too that I am a career diplomat, at the service of Ghana and Ghana alone.

"I want to believe that the reason we are where we are in terms of positions we occupy in the Ghanaian political system is because we each have something good, something positive to offer to our fatherland. Whatever your choice, think of that. God bless you."

Chapter Fifteen

L ike his colleague, Kwesi Armah's position was clear: he too was obviously for the new regime. Perhaps some other persons were still to speak, perhaps not, but there was an interruption. Quaison's table telephone rang twice. He picked up the receiver while everybody looked on.

"Yes, Mr. President," he was heard saying. "Yes, Mr. President. Right away Mr. President." He then looked nervously round the room as if to see it somebody had leaked the minutes of their meeting to the President.

"The President wants to address us all, in his conference room," he announced. Members of the President's personal secretariat were called in, so also were some members of his personal security corps.

***

While Bossman and Kwesi Armah stayed behind to get everybody together so that they go in as one bunch, Quaison went ahead to set the stage and prepare for their coming. Nkrumah's door was not shut, it was ajar. Inadvertently peeping through the opening between the shutter and the wall he noticed that the President was sitting at his table in a pair of grey knee-long pants and a sleeveless singlette of the same colour. He had never seen the President in that "naked" attire. At home if he must receive a visitor, Nkrumah always wore his down reaching dressing gown. Thinking that the President may have been caught off guard, considering the lateness of the hour, he cleared his throat to announce his presence at the door. Then he knocked.

"Come inside," the President said without noticing that there was anything amiss.

Quaison entered the room and immediately asked:

"Can my people come, Osagyefo?"

"Sure, show them in."

Quaison scratched his head nervously and then said: "Osagyefo will receive them like that?"

Osagyefo smacked his lips and said: "Yes, Osagyefo will receive them like this, naked. Osagyefo is naked. Of course he is. What need does he have for accoutrements anymore? Stripped of his *élan vital*, stripped of the presidency of Ghana, Osagyefo must be naked. Ghana is even more naked," he said as he moved towards the wardrobe and pulled his overcoat. "Ghana without Osagyefo is a naked country."

Quaison helped him put on the coat as his continued with his soliloquy. He then went into the small conference room and made sure that the sitting arrangement was fine. He was merely interested in the position of the large armchair in which his president would sit. He went and called the rest of his team in. After they had taken their places he went for the President. When he entered they all rose and greeted with the usual idolatrous appellations and attributes which in everybody's ears now sounded like mockery:

"Osagyefo! Kantamanto! Star of Africa! Man of Destiny!"

He waved to them to sit down. Just as he was in the habit of doing, Nkrumah did not give anybody the opportunity to suggest anything. Like the captain of a sinking ship amidst mutinous crew, as if the only thing worth considering or listening to, was what he thought and said, he began his now all-too-familiar diatribe. He spoke like a radio that had been suddenly turned on in the midst of a broadcast, without preamble:

"We shall measure our progress by the improvement in the health of our people; by the number of children in school, and by the quality of their education; by the availability of water and electricity in our towns and villages, and by the happiness which our people take in being able to manage their own affairs. The welfare of our people is our chief pride, and it is by this that my government will ask to be judged.

"Fellow-countrymen and women, this afternoon I told you that the traitorous Army-Police rebellion in Ghana was instigated and prompted by neo-colonialist enemies of Ghana and Africa. These enemies know my unflinching stand against imperialism and neo-colonialism. Ghana has always been feared and hated by the imperialists and the neo-colonialists. Immediately after independence, I declared that Ghana's independence was meaningless unless it was linked up with the total liberation of Africa. Today, no less than 36 African states have also won their political independence...

"In Ghana, our state-owned factories and industries, state and co-operative farms and enterprises, and our gigantic Volta River complex have placed us in a position to industrialize and revolutionalise our agriculture. This is the sure way to set about to achieve our economic independence. That is why, to the imperialists and the neo-colonialists, Ghana has become too dangerous an example to the rest of Africa to be allowed to continue under its socialist leadership. According to their specious logic, Ghana, in the forefront of the struggle for a free and united Africa and on the brink of a great industrial breakthrough which would have given true economic independence, had become too dangerous an example to the rest of Africa to be allowed to continue under a socialist-directed governmental system such as I had put in place.

"Since independence, our enemies have spared no effort in persistently and continuously undermining and sabotaging our progress and development. They have planned and sponsored by bribery and corruption and intrigues to capture and destroy Ghana's economy. They have consistently tried to find stooges and lackeys to do their dirty jobs for them. Finally, I say finally, they have found the expected tools in the so-called Notorious Liars Council which they think is a National Liberation Council.

"I appeal to you as the brains which I chose from 8 million Ghanaians, to serve me in this crusade against neo-colonialist/imperialist infiltration and domination of Africa in general and Ghana in particular, not to be a party to it. We must stand firm in our resolve to right the wrong that has been committed back home in Ghana. We will travel back to Africa as the one family that left Ghana, even though our mission has been aborted. We shall visit the corridors of power across the world as one family and we shall plead our case until such a time that we find it propitious for us to land in Ghana and continue our great task from where we left off. Forward Ever," he said, raising his voice defiantly through the dark, silent night.

There was a long silence and then some slight cross-talk until Quaison raised his hand. The President was about to talk again. He talked of motions of solidarity he continues to receive from friendly leaders such as Nasser of Egypt, Julius Nyerere of Tanzania, Modibo Keita of Mali, and Sekou Touré of Guinea amongst others. In particular, he decided to read Sekou Touré's message to him:

The political Bureau and the Government after a thorough analysis of the African situation following the seizure of power by the instruments of imperialism have decided:

1. Organize a national day of solidarity with the Ghanaian people next Sunday. Throughout the length and breadth of the country there will take place popular demonstrations on the theme of anti-imperialism.

2. To call on all progressive African countries to hold a special conference and take all adequate measures. We think that the time factor is vital here, since it is important to make a riposte without delay, by every means. Your immediate presence would be very opportune it seems to us, and we are therefore impatiently waiting for you."

"Isn't it nice that in trying times such as these we find friends on whom we can easily count on" he asked, looking round the hall. Some people were not even listening to or looking in his direction.

"Quaison," he turned to his Minister of Foreign Affairs.

"Osagyefo," the man jerked to attention.

"Your ticket, plus five hundred pounds. You leave for Addis Ababa tomorrow to attend the OAU Council of Ministers. You will represent the CPP. You will find enclosed suggestions which you are free to modify for your presentation."

"Yes, Osagyefo."

"Bossman," he turned to his ambassador in UK, "You will leave for the UK tomorrow and await fresh instructions from me. Your package is also ready."

"Yes, Osagyefo."

"And the rest of us, we leave for Guinea Conakry via Moscow on the 28th. No time to lose. I can't wait to eat my Ghanaian *fou fou* and *aponchi* again and eat my *kenke*," he added on a lighter note. "Tomorrow I shall hold a press conference at which everything would be put in proper perspective. Any questions?"

There was a hand up. It was the hand of Ambrose Yankey. Reluctantly Nkrumah beckoned on him to speak. The man moved slightly to the front. He was just of average height, but with rather unkempt features and a belly that hung over his belt like a sack of an overgrown water melon.

He spoke rather indistinctly, such that it was not very easy to hear him from a distance. Initially his language power was embarrassing and he could mix up tense in free variation while making his point. But, over the years, and as a result of constant practice his semi-illiterate status had improved tremendously or virtually disappeared. A great snuff taker, he had a lifetime affliction that always made him look comical. Whenever he rose to speak, he would sneeze, clean his nostrils from which sometimes unawares, a thin line of moist snuff would trickle down unpicturesquely. And then almost immediately, the comedy started: he would stop speaking, close his eyes, contort his entire face as if to explode into another sneeze, but the sneeze would disappear, only to threaten again and again later. He had large, bulging eyes like those of a dragonfly that were capable of all sorts of expressions. He commanded the least respect amongst his colleagues. But, until the coup, Nkrumah regarded him very highly. He stammered:

"Has Osagyefo considered any other alternative to this decision?"

"Which decision and alternative to what/"

"I mean the alternative to going to Guinea, Osagefo."

"Osagyefo has considered all alternatives," Nkrumah retorted looking at the man with malevolent eyes. "What alternative were you considering?"

Ambrose Yankey cleared his throat. "In 1960, Osagyefo," the man began timidly but as if to impress his listeners, "when the Emperor Haile Selaisie was almost toppled by a military coup like this, he went straight back home and chased away the soldiers and so nothing else happened."

"Is that all?"

"That's all, Osagyefo."

"Next question," Nkrumah turned away from the god that had failed him, to the silent amusement of the other senior members of the entourage.

Chapter Sixteen

On Friday February 27th Nkrumah very reluctantly decided to hold a 'general press conference'. He did it *reluctantly* because, unlike the interviews which he was used to holding with the Ghanaian press and journalists, he could neither predict nor influence what they would ask him. The Ghanaian journalists whom he had so thoroughly subjugated lived in terror of him and knew the risks involved in asking questions which would elicit nothing but his greatness and personal achievements, questions which could embarrass the President. They always knew what he liked to hear and gave him exactly that. Out there in Hanoi, it would have been a different matter if the peace mission had succeeded because he would have been talking only about it to journalists. But the mission had been aborted and worse still, he had been overthrown. This meant that any interview would have to centre mainly around the subject of his fall from grace – something he would not like to talk about. He was then condemned to face the western press which he had so often likened to "houseflies because they pass off our pleasant parts to dwell only on our wounds!"

Even more than this was the fact that unknown to him, he was completely isolated. And this isolation, accentuated or compounded by a moral blindness which prompted him to dwell only on his past glories produced a picture of complete ridicule. A BBC reporter at the press conference described him well when he likened him to the king in Hans Christian Andersen's tale in which the fact that he was naked and ridiculous was apparent to all in his kingdom but himself.

Just how appropriate this metaphor was lay in the fact that while Nkrumah's radio and TV remained shut, much water had gone under the bridge: his Minister of Defence and political protégé for eighteen years, Kofi Baako had been shown over Ghanaian TV condemning him. "It pained me to realize that Nkrumah was not a genuine leader but a fraud of the highest order," the former minister had said. Also appearing on Ghanaian TV monitored from Peking were declarations of three key members of his entourage – Quaison Sackey (who was supposed to be on his way to represent the CPP at the Foreign Ministers' Conference at Addis Ababa), Dei-Anang (his closest adviser on African Affairs), and J.E. Boss (Ambassador to the UK). All three announced that they had already deserted Nkrumah and had asked for (and had been granted)asylum from the Chinese Government.

Quaison Sackey had even made a joke of his historical role! Asked whether he thought he would be admitted into the new regime in the same manner that he had served under Nkrumah, Quaison Sackey was quoted as saying: "Nkrumah made me a key member of his team because he saw that I was a good player. A good player will always find a good spot in a good team." The same defection had been announced by many other members of the Hanoi peace mission, a fact which Nkrumah would discover only at the point of departure for Africa the next day.

***

Yet, in spite of this, he needed to make a statement to the world about the coup. He needed to rally his supporters back home in Ghana and the only means of doing so was by talking to the press. Shortly before midday the stage was set: the same hall in which the banquet had taken place the previous evening was prepared for the purpose. Pressmen and photographers occupied the front row of about twenty five seats. There were six microphones mounted on the dais, through which he addressed the audience of some three hundred personalities. Many of the pressmen did not ask questions, they simply held up their tape recorders to record both the questions asked and the answers delivered. They would develop them in their various ways into full-length articles. Each time a journalist rose to ask a question he introduced himself and the organisation he represented.

Answering to the question on his next move now that he had been removed from office and he had cancelled the peace mission, Nkrumah declared that he was going back to Africa.

"How safe is it for you to land in Ghana at this point in time?" he was asked.

"We are not returning to Ghana," he said. "We would be going first to Guinea before working out our next move."

"Why Guinea? If you are so anxious to return and meet your people and, if you are so sure that your people are anxiously waiting for you, don't you think it would make more sense to return to Ghana rather than elsewhere, irrespective of its proximity to Ghana?"

"It could have been anywhere else," Nkrumah said. "I have invitations to Tanzania from Julius Nyerere, to Egypt from my father-in-law, Gamel Nasser, to Mali from Modibo Keita, and the like." He then read out the invitation from Sekou Touré and then added: "We need to regroup, outside Ghana, before advancing."

The journalist went on:

"You have cancelled your all-important peace mission to Hanoi and it is more than likely that your party will not have sorted out things sufficiently to feature at the OAU Council of Ministers in Addis Ababa. Do you not see that you are losing a lot of ground already? You seem to imply that somewhere in the deep recesses of your mind, you think that the coup has succeeded."

"Instead it is you journalists who are sending out the wrong signal. You are the ones creating the impression that it has succeeded," Nkrumah said. "We are not losing any ground. My Foreign Minister has been assigned that particular mission: He will attend the Council of Ministers' meeting in Addis Ababa. There he will present the CPP's government's position. And he is a dependable man when it comes to that."

"Anybody looking at the jubilant crowds and soldiers in every major city in Ghana cannot help but conclude that the coup is succeeding or has succeeded."

"What are you calling jubilant crowds in every big city in Ghana/" Nkrumah inquired with subdued fury. "Ghana has a population of nine million inhabitants. If the western TVs choose to move the images of a handful of relatives of the traitors from Tamale to Accra, Kumasi and Takoradi, and you choose to call that jubilant crowds in every big city, then I feel sorry for you. It is like saying that it was a *bloodless* coup. Yes, that's what the British and American presses are saying. And my sources tell me that at least 2000 Ghanaians have been killed. That doesn't sound *bloodless* to me. At least 200 soldiers have been killed at Flagstaff House alone. And you of the BBC say it was bloodless."

As matter of fact, there was gross exaggeration of the size and strength of 'favourable' reaction in Ghana. Obviously, there were some who welcomed the change, namely Opposition elements hostile to the CPP. Then there were relatives and friends of those released from prison, political and criminal detainees. Maximum publicity was given to their demonstrations of joy, and to the pulling down of Nkrumah's statue outside the Parliament building in Accra. In addition, there was a section of market traders who had suffered as a result of the *Abrahams Report*, which had exposed malpractices. There were opportunists and the genuinely misled who thought the coup would usher in a new era devoid of shortages of consumer goods and other problems associated with the implementation of CPP development plans, coupled with the disastrous fall in the world price of cocoa.

These details were new to the BBC reporter who looked disturbed, but remained undaunted. However, he continued:

"Let's go back to the Addis Ababa Conference."

"What about it?"

"You talked of having sent your foreign minister to represent you…"

"Yes I did…"

"But what if the coup plotters also send a representative," the journalist continued, "wouldn't it look ridiculous to have two representatives with diametrically opposed views at the same conference?"

Nkrumah responded:

"I have told you that this headache is being caused by an infinitesimal minority of misguided subversionists with no agenda to offer for Ghana or Africa, either politically or economically. How can they show up? What would they be going there to say? They can never have Economic and Financial Advisers. No right-thinking Ghanaian intellectual can condescend to sell his talents at so low a price as to side with them."

Then with the usual folly and arrogance of politicians in newly independent states who assume that because they have played their part in winning independence their people owe them an everlasting debt which will excuse corruption, extravagance, nepotism and arbitrary rule, Nkrumah said:

"Take me out of the scene and it would have taken Ghana back by 500 years in an effort to catch up with the pace I have set, if only to try and fail. The Chairman of the clique is Ankra, an officer we dismissed not so long ago, for incompetence. The only thing I see them doing very well is to send for Lyndon Johnson or his accomplice, Harold Wilson, to represent them…."

"But those are not Ghanaians, Mr. President," another journalist pointed out.

"Of course I know that," Nkrumah admitted with a gentle smile of confidence. "But I also know those are the human figures pulling the strings from behind the curtain which make those neo-colonialist imperialist marionettes behave the way they do. Without those bastards fanning from the background there would be no trouble in Ghana today. Take it from me, and I challenge you to investigate thorough: Ghana is no longer being run by an African government. It is being administered by a small clique of illiterate army and police officers, and behind the Ghanaian façade, the decisions are being made by foreign interests."

"Mr. President," a journalist who introduced himself as a BBC reporter for Peking began, "supposing, I say supposing, these so-called traitors stand their ground and make it impossible for you to regain your presidency, what legacy shall you have left for Ghana? Or is it that most of your great ideas had not yet been given practical implementation?"

Nkrumah, at first thought he should refuse to respond to any questions from such an accomplice. But he changed his mind, took in a deep, long breath and then declared:

"I don't ever want to consider that impossibility. Never. I am Kantamanto, remember?" he said boastfully, but without visible conviction. "I am Ghana, I am the alpha and the omega of Ghana and of all Africa. I am either President of Ghana or there would be no Ghana. What political experience does any of these imps have to step into Osagyefo's shoes? Let me give them 48 hours and they will come begging on their knees. If it were not for the great harm, the enormity of the harm it does to Ghanaians, my people, my children, we could find this laughable. It is interesting and at the same time ridiculous, that this clique of army and police adventurers should call themselves a

"National Liberation Council". What have they liberated, and what are they trying to liberate? Or do they believe that they are liberating Ghana in order to make a present to their imperialist and neo-colonialist masters? I would advise this clique of lying traitors rather to liberate themselves first from their neo-colonialist and imperialist masters. It makes me want to cry instead."

The BBC journalist nodded but insisted:

"Mr. President, how would you rate yourself on a ten point scale?"

Nkrumah did not like the idea of thinking of him as somebody who had come to the end of his journey. "You do not stop a long distance runner in the middle of a race to ask him to rate himself. I am only at the beginning of my mission in this continent. As I said during independence, Ghana's independence is meaningless unless it is linked to the total liberation of the African continent. I have just embarked on that. When all shall have been said and done, it is history that will rate me."

"But you should be able to rate yourself even at this early stage."

"My achievements are there for the world to see," he began and then as ever, went into amazing details as if reading from a book. "At independence, Ghana inherited almost complete trade dependence on West. The economy was mainly foreign or locally capitalist owned. A colonial mentality permeated the professions, the army, police, and civil service. For the record, and as I said before, 'Those who would judge me merely by the heights we have would do well to remember the depths from which we started.'

"I had to start virtually from scratch when the First Development Plan was launched. The First and Second year Development Plans covered the periods 1951-56 and 1954-64, and the Consolation Plan bridged the two year gap between these plans (1957-59). Then in March 1964, building on the foundations of the previous Plans, the Seven Year Development Plan was launched. Our aim, under that Plan, was to build in Ghana a socialist state which accepts full responsibility for promoting the well-being of the masses."

Chapter Seventeen

Here he mopped the sweat from his forehead, and drank a full glass of mineral water before going on tirelessly:

"My long-term objective of the socialist state I was building in Ghana was to be achieved by stages. There was to be a period of mixed economy when a limited private sector would be allowed to operate and when vigorous public and co-operative sectors would rapidly expand, particularly in the strategic productive areas of the economy. Eventually, with the full implementation of Development Plans, the private sector was to be eventually eliminated.

"The very first programme of my CPP, contained in the party constitution drawn up in 1949, clearly stated that the objective was the establishment of a 'socialist state in which all men and women shall have equal opportunity and where there shall be no capitalist exploitation.' Later, in the Party's *Programme for Work and Happiness* launched in 1962, it was again declared that 'the principles upon which the party is pivoted' were those of socialism. The main tasks of the Plan were: firstly to speed up the rate of growth of our national economy. Secondly, it was to enable us to embark upon the socialist transformation of our economy through the rapid development of the state and co-operative sector. Thirdly, it was our aim, by this Plan, to eradicate completely the colonial structure of our economy.

"I was to develop a self-sustaining economy, balanced between industry and agriculture, providing a sufficiency of food for the people, and supporting secondary industries based on the products of our agriculture. In other words, Ghana's economy was to be diversified in order to lessen the heavy dependence on cocoa, and to develop the infrastructure necessary for industrialization and for the achievement of a satisfactory level of integration of industry and agriculture. My people, through the state, were to have an effective share in the economy of the country and an effective control over it.

"During the period 1951-64 I had already laid the foundations for a modern state. A network of roads, considered to be among the most modern in Africa was constructed. Houses, schools, colleges, hospitals, clinics were built. Many state enterprises and corporations were set up, and a State Management Committee established to supervise them. At this moment that I am talking to you, there sixty-three enterprises in existence. Among the new industries founded were two cocoa-processing plants, two sugar refineries, a textile printing plant, a glass factory, a chocolate factory, a radio assembly plant, a meat-processing plant and a large printing works at Tema. In addition, work has well advanced on a gold refinery at Tarkwa, asbestos, cement, shoe and rubber tyre factories at Kumasi, and a factory for the manufacture of prefabricated houses. Ghana is beginning to supply local demand for many basic consumer goods, using locally-produced raw materials….

"Look at what I have done in the field of education! In the first ten years of my administration, I have achieved more in education than during the whole period of colonial rule. The education Act of 1961 I made education compulsory for school-age children. All education from primary to university level is free. In addition, all textbooks are supplied free to pupils in primary, middle and secondary schools. As of this moment, Ghana has one of the highest literacy rates in Africa, among the best public services and the highest living standards *per capita* in Africa.

"I stand corrected, but, as far as I know, for the very first time in Africa, I made it possible for women to be appointed to serve on boards of corporations, schools and town councils. Those that we found impressive enough were chosen to serve on the Central Committee of the CPP. Increasing numbers of women entered courses of higher education, many pursuing training courses abroad qualifying them to occupy most of the positions previously held exclusively by men. In addition, discriminatory provisions relating to women's work were abolished, and equal pay instituted for equal work. Maternity leave on full pay was assured. Women underwent pilot training in the Ghana Air Force Training School at Takoradi. Women were encouraged to enrol in the army to train alongside men in the infantry, in the intelligence and service corps, and to become electrical and mechanical engineers.

"As regards industrialization, there were three broad aspects of CPP development plans. First, industries were to be established which would be large consumers of power and for which raw materials would be locally available. Second, there were to be industries which would utilize cash crops, and which would provide employment in rural areas. Third, light industries were to be set up for the production of such goods as textiles, shoes, clothing and furniture. For each programme of industrialization, hydro-electric power had to be provided on a massive scale, and this was the purpose of the Volta River Project. When I described the Volta Dam as 'the greatest of all our development projects' I meant every word of what I said. The project was designed to make possible the development of' the full industrial potential of Ghana and the provisions of power for neighbouring states. Ghana was estimated to have sufficient bauxite to last for 200 years, and this would be processed by a new aluminium smelter at Tema using Volta hydroelectric power. The initial power output of the Volta Dam was estimated at (512, 000kw at full load), and for the ultimate power output at 768,000kw (882,000kw at full load). The giant scheme, which cost £70 million to complete was financed 50 per cent by Ghana. The rest of the money was provided by raising international loans.

"As I foresaw it, the electrification of Ghana was to make possible the building of a modern industrialized state whose citizens would also be able to enjoy the domestic benefits which the provision of electricity would provide. It was my dream that every house in Ghana would soon have electric light. It is in view of all these achievements that I found it hard to admit that a coup had overthrown me in Ghana. In Ghana? What did Ghanaians expect me to have done? And that explains why I think the coup could only have been staged by some persons who feel uncomfortable by the rate at which I have developed Ghana.

"Even before the inauguration of the Volta River Project last month, I had published a thoroughgoing exposure of the operations of international companies in my book, *Neo-colonialism: The Last Stage of Imperialism*. There I stated in black and white that

The essence of neo-colonialism is that the state which is subject to it is, in theory independent and has all the outward trappings of international sovereignty. In reality, its economic system and thus its political policy is directed from outside. In that my book which infuriated the US Government so much that they immediately cancelled a $35 million aid which had been promised us, I remember saying that the less developed world will not become developed through the good will or generosity of the developed powers. It can only become developed through a struggle against the external forces which have a vested interest in keeping it underdeveloped.

"Mr. President, you must have a terrific memory to remember all that so accurately," the journalist pointed out, drawing impressive nods from everybody, and a slight applause from some quarters. And then the journalist pressed on, "but why would you publish such a book, knowing that it was bound to anger the US and other superpowers?"

"Thanks for the compliment. I remember everything that I have done as well as written because I felt it to my bones and marrow at the time I wrote it or did it. I felt them like labour pains and absolutely had to get them out of my mind to remain healthy. And back to the point, my intention was not to hurt the Americans," Nkrumah said tongue-in-cheek. "It only occurred to me that it was necessary for me to spotlight the workings of the multi-national corporations in Africa based on my own practical experience as head of a government engaged on a socialist path of development. In compiling it I simply thought that it was important to make available to the African people an analysis of the workings of neo-colonialism and how it could be overcome. Although the activities of multinationals operating in Ghana were not even as widespread as elsewhere in Africa, their very presence tended to undermine my government. I therefore wrote it in self-defence."

"These achievements that you have just enumerated sound very impressive indeed, coming from you. But I find it hard to reconcile these successes with the declaration made over TV and radio by the Chairman of the NLC in Ghana…"

"And what declaration are you referring to?" Nkrumah asked with subdued fury.

"They keep saying that they took up arms against you in order to save Ghana from economic chaos."

Nkrumah threw his hands open to the journalists and the audience. "All the successes I have just mentioned above, do they sound like achievements that can be forged in a national economy in a state of chaos?" Nkrumah queried.

The journalist kept quiet.

"No, you answer me sincerely."

"Certainly not," Nkrumah cut in before the man had time to answer. And then he added: "There can never be a bigger lie anywhere on this planet – that Ghana needed to be rescued from economic chaos! And if you believe that you can believe anything. The bitter truth is that the fabrication of such a blatant lie was essential in the planning of any usurpation of power. Various other lies are hinged to this central lie. The country was said to be hopelessly in debt and the people at the verge of starvation. Among the lies aimed against me personally was the one that I had accumulated a large personal fortune; this was to form the basis for an all-out character assassination attempt. But these lies were subsidiary to the one big lie of 'economic mismanagement', which is to provide an umbrella excuse for the seizure of power by Kotoka, Ankrah and the other neo-colonialist inspired traitors.

"If Ghana was in such a serious economic condition, why was there no lack of investment in her growing industries? Investors do not put their money into obviously mismanaged enterprises and unstable economies. And by the way, who made up the figures of Ghana's supposed debt? They talk of unnecessary waste and expenditure. How can the obvious evidence of the modernisation and industrialisation of Ghana, such as the new roads, factories, schools and hospitals, the harbour and town of Tema, the Volta and Teffle bridges and the Volta dam be reconciled with the charge of wasted expenditure? So you see that it is the reverse that is true: I have been overthrown because I have succeeded beyond neo-colonialist expectations. Next question please."

"And now that you are so confident of going back to continue from where you had stopped," another journalist pressed on, "what do you intend to do with the plotters? Try them for high treason or something of the sort?"

"I don't even expect to find them still in Ghana," Nkrumah told him confidently, "those overgrown babies! They were seeking for notice and nothing else. What has taken place in Ghana is not a *coup d'état* but a rebellion and it is going to be crushed by its own actions. There is a Russian proverb that one cannot screen the sun by the palm of a hand. I will want first of all to know the root cause. I would like to understand those who permitted their bodies to be used and abused by those neo-colonialist imperialists."

The journalist nodded as he made his notes and then looked round. There was another hand up. Nkrumah asked the man to go ahead.

"Mr President, members of the NLC have claimed as a major reason for taking up arms against you the fact that you have not only ridiculed Ghana and Ghanaians with failures in your foreign policies but have placed the army at an unprecedented and severe risk by reducing innocent Ghanaians who were recruited or who offered to be recruited in order to serve and protect their fatherland to cannon fodder in pointless international struggles which even you yourself could see that you would never emerge victorious."

"Can you explain what you mean by that? What foreign policies could they be talking about, for example?"

"They mentioned, in particular, the case of your clash with Belgium in connection with the Congo, Britain in connection with Rhodesia and South Africa, Portugal in connection with Mozambique, Angola, and Namib…"

Nkrumah did not even allow the man to finish talking. Nkrumah never had a kind word for the coup plotters. Wagging a finer of complete condemnation and refutation, he told the journalist:

"As I have been saying since I heard of that their child's play which they are calling a coup in Ghana, it is the work of numskulls who on their own are not only blind, but incapable of noticing or appreciating the great historical transformation which I am engaged in. I am talking about empty vessels being fed by the panicky outcry of frightened neo-colonialists organisations. You can now see their ignorance manifesting itself. Anybody who thinks I made a mistake in sending troops to the Congo has no idea of what I stood for. At our own independence, when I said that the independence of Ghana would be meaningless unless it was followed by the total liberation of the entire African continent from foreign domination, I meant exactly that. It was not electoral propaganda. I had already secured some kind of unity with Guinea, Mali and Togoland. All those places they have mentioned as areas where I carried out unnecessary intervention are places on the African soil that were under the kind of foreign domination which needed to be eradicated. Is there any need to stress to you what independence of the Congo must mean to every African leader who regards the freedom and prosperity of the whole African continent as indivisible? Politically, strategically and economically, the Congo is a most vital region of Africa. Foreign powers which have concerned themselves with what they like to call 'the defence of Africa' – by which they mean the defence on the African continent, of interests which are mainly contrary to those of the African people – clearly regard the Congo as the key to the military control of Africa. Thus, in my considered opinion, the degree of the Congo's independence was bound to substantially determine the ultimate fate of the whole continent of Africa.

"When Patrice Lumumba, Congo's first Prime Minister, visited Ghana in 1960 we worked out some kind of entente…"

"What kind of entente, Mr. President?"

"Some kind of union on the basis of which Ghana would come to his aid in case of trouble which I could see looming in the horizon."

"And vice versa, Mr. President?"

"And vice versa," Nkrumah admitted.

"Did the President not consider the fact that such a union was bound to run into difficulties, given the distance that separates the two countries?"

Nkrumah hesitated for a while before saying:

"Indeed, distance was considered a crucial factor, but not a deterrent. In fact, distance had very little to do with the problems we faced there. You would be surprised to hear that it was going to be a more feasible union than the others I had forged with the West African states near me. The cause of the crisis lay in the fact that suddenly, and as I had feared, I noticed that the colonial powers had re-entrenched themselves in the Congo. First I learnt that President Kasavubu had expelled the Ghanaian Ambassador, and that he had dismissed Patrice Lumumba as Prime Minister. This was a severe blow to my personal integrity and everything that I stood for, considering that Kasavubu was a puppet that had been set up to create confusion so that the Belgians, the CIA, and Britain could exploit the confusion to their economic advantage which obviously meant owning the enormously profitable Congolese mines, especially the rich copper and uranium mines in Katanga Province.

"I mention these details because they show the nefarious workings of the imperialists to undermine African stability. Both the Belgians and the CIA relied on the Chief of Staffs of the Congolese Army, a Sergeant Joseph-Désiré Mobutu. (The Belgians had recruited him as an agent of their secret service and then promoted him straight from sergeant to colonel; later, when the US became the prime Western mover in the Congo, the Belgians passed him on to the CIA as their main Congolese "asset"!) His job was to harass Lumumba and they eventually got Mobutu to place Lumumba under house arrest. Then the Belgian/CIA coalition instigated Kasavubu to declare in September 1960 that he had "sacked" Lumumba as Prime Minister.

"Kasavubu's action was illegal, for Lumumba had been elected Prime Minister by the Congolese parliament, in which Lumumba's Congolese National Movement (MNC) held the largest number of seats. It was his party that had appointed Kasavubu president, not vice versa. But the Belgian/CIA coalition knew that if Kasavubu "sacked" Lumumba, the chaos in the Congo would get worse, and Lumumba's position would become untenable.

"Angered by Kasavubu's unconstitutional action, Lumumba also "dismissed" Kasavubu. Governments and foreign companies alike were being urged to choose which "government" of the Congo to do business with. I called on the United Nations to restore Lumumba to power. But the UN command in Leopoldville (now Kinshasa) was headed by an American, Andrew Cordier. You can guess what happened: on instructions from the CIA, Cordier – the supposedly neutral representative of the UN Secretary-General in Leopoldville-ordered UN troops to close all Congolese airports to all traffic other than that of the UN. This prevented Lumumba from being able to fly in troop reinforcements, crucially needed in Leopoldville to buttress his position in the capital, from Katanga, where they had been sent to crush the Belgian-inspired secessionist attempt by Moise Tshombe. Again, on the orders of Andrew Cordier, a UN official went to Radio Congo and had the radio crystal removed, just when Lumumba needed to broadcast to his supporters to alert them to what Kasavubu was up to. Lumumba was thus forced into radio silence, while Kasavubu, helped by his Western bosses, was able to broadcast on Radio Brazzaville, the powerful French-owned radio station just across the river, in Congo-Brazzaville.

Chapter Eighteen

The Chinese government provided the plane that was to take Nkrumah and whatever was left of his entourage to Moscow and thence to Africa. The departure time was 8 o'clock in the morning of February 28. By 6 o'clock, the reporting time, nobody amongst his senior ministers had yet made an appearance. Not even the Ghanaian Ambassador to Peking who had been with him since his arrival. He did not remember seeing any of them at the press conference the previous afternoon. Not that they were supposed to be there, but common courtesy required that they sit around just to give him moral support. The only person who continued to hang around him like an albatross was Ambrose Yankey. There was something he had tried to tell Nkrumah since the previous evening. But because of the fact that he had not covered Nkrumah sufficiently, Nkrumah did not seem to pay any attention.

"If you have anything to say," he told Yankey more than once, "wait until we arrive Conakry."

Had Nkrumah given Yankey the chance to talk, he would have known ere long that the key members of his entourage had already absconded, that they, including the Ghanaian Ambassador, had asked for and had been granted asylum. Finding that the only person to listen to him that early morning was Ambrose Yankey he had been forced to ask the man where the others were. It was then that Nkrumah learnt the truth.

"But it cannot be," Nkrumah shouted and then sent for the Chinese Premier. When the old man came, he confirmed Nkrumah's fears.

"Why would you grant asylum to my entire entourage without my consent?" he queried.

"That is a question that can only be answered by the Minister of Interior," the man replied. "But I guess he knows that Ghana and China have a bilateral agreement, and so we could not have denied them that request, given the state of things in Ghana now."

Nkrumah tried to talk but words stuck in his throat and he only swallowed and kept quiet. After a while he turned to Yankey:

"Did you say Quaison has abandoned me?"

"He has, Osagyefo."

"And Bossman? And Kwesi Armah? And the women too?"

"All of them, Osagyefo. They were all shown on TV declaring support for the coup. That is what I was trying to say since yesterday but Osagyefo did not want to see me," the man ended up.

"But you should have told me that that was what you wanted to say," Nkrumah told him. And then in a beguiling and rare fit of self-deprecation he said to the Chinese Premier: "I was a bird flying high in the sky. That news of the coup shot me in the wing. This news of mass defections of my personal friends, has shot me in the other wing. Why would they be granted asylum, Mr. Prime Minister, seeing my predicament?"

"Even yourself," the old man went on, "if you ask for asylum we wouldn't hesitate to grant it."

"Maybe you are thinking of a lunatic asylum," Nkrumah said almost to himself. And so he had to leave for Moscow with only a fraction, twenty one to be exact, of his original sixty-six man team. That number would swell to eighty after they were joined by Ghanaian students and some freedom fighters who, inspired by his philosophy, had gone to study in Russia. From the look of things, he knew his end was near, or at least not as far as such.

Chapter Nineteen

On 27 April 1972, Kwame Nkrumah died in a hospital in Bucharest, Romania. Given the circumstances surrounding his life following his overthrow, (as attested by his faithful servant, Ambrose Yankey who was closest to him until he left for Romania), the wonder was not that he died at all, but that he even managed to live for that long. After the discovery of the mass defections in the morning of their departure from Peking, Nkrumah had rethought his sidelining of Ambrose Yankey and had decided to take him back into his full confidence. He had reconsidered the fact that Yankey who would have been very welcomed by the NLC for the role they all knew he played in Nkrumah's life, had every reason to have defected like the others. But he had chosen not to do so but to remain and die with his master. He reconsidered the fact that the overthrow could not have been blamed on a mortal like Yankey. After all, he concluded, he too must take part of the blame because on that fateful morning of 22 February at the Accra airport prior to their departure, he too had failed to obey his natural instincts when he had changed his mind after having actually climbed down to call off the trip. In Yankey's words, when news came that on the 13 January 1972 that Colonel Ignatius Kutu Acheampong had overthrown Dr. Kofi Abrefa Busia's government which had been in power in Ghana since 1969, Nkrumah did not look excited. Instead, he is said to have told Yankey:

"Too little too late. I see nothing but treachery everywhere. Every single person that he once counted on let him down or was forced by circumstances to let him down, just at the moment that he most needed their support."

When told that the coup leaders had stretched an invitation to him to return to Ghana, Nkrumah had asked:

"To die or to rule?"

"To rule of course," Yankey had told him.

Nkrumah is said to have uttered a long grating laugh at the end of which he had gone into a litany of woes he had encountered:

"How can they turn back the clock? Fate has brought me too far down to rise again. I have never had any accounts in foreign banks. My account in Barclays Bank into which my presidential salary had been paid was frozen by the NLC. I think other African leaders will learn their lesson. I have been dependent entirely on the generosity of political friends. That is not good for a mighty titan like myself, Osagyefo, a man who by the snap of the finger could make ten thousand pounds available to a needy friend."

Here he was referring to an instant loan of £10m he had granted Sekou Touré when the colonial master, France, in an immense seizure of pique, took away every movable object in the country because Guinea refused to become "second-class French citizens" and opted for independence!

"And then, and then, my dear Ambrose, the degree of mistrust, treachery and betrayal which I have come to associate with Ghanaians in particular and humanity in general, is such that I am better off dying than living with it. It is true that when I arrived in Conakry on 2 March 1966, six days after my overthrow, I was made a co-president of Guinea by President Sekou Touré, and I was seen by many Guineans as very deserving of the co-presidential honour bestowed on me at that large political rally in Conakry. It is also true that Sekou my *pan-Africanist brother*, made me the co-secretary-general of the ruling PDG party, and settled us so comfortably in Villa Syli.

"But I am telling you from the bottom of my heart that none of these favours could ever salvage my crushed ego. As our people say, Ambrose, a dog barks loudest only in its own backyard. Like a bee that gets its sting from its hive, without Ghana, my policies are meaningless. Ghana was the laboratory from which my theories were manufactured. My books merely interpreted them in the light of what I was doing there. Here in Guinea we are all of us strangers. Do you speak French?"

"Well, just a little, Osagyefo. I try my best."

"At least you try. I do not speak it, I do not understand it, I do not write it. And yet I am co-president and things of the sort. Even a child can see that all these favours were just to placate me because I was their benefactor."

Here he paused for a long while before asking:

"How could all those my African friends of the OAU not raise an army and march into Ghana and chase away the riffraffs and reinstate me? How could we leave my return to chance?"

Based on his own knowledge of the way Nkrumah regarded himself, Ambrose Yankey declared rightly that allegations, suspicions and conspiracy theories surrounding his last days in Conakry, must be discounted in favour of the severe damage the feeling of betrayal must have had on him as a human being, as President of Ghana and founder of the OAU. Something snapped inside him on that 24th February 1966 which could never be repaired, even with the publication of so many books.

Yankey himself a semi-illiterate, said that some of those who liked to sympathise with him would normally say that his removal from office was a God-sent blessing because it then gave him an opportunity to write the many books he wrote, and which have more lasting and enduring effects on mankind than his physical presence at the helm of Ghanaian politics. But it must be remembered that the obsessional preoccupation with the writing of the books only came to complement his fame as President. They did not replace his historical role.

It is, he added, like saying a hunter who has missed his chance of tracking down game should be satisfied with writing a book on how to track down game. Or, again, it would be like a boxer, a world title contender, who when he is knocked out decides to write books about winning the title in the delusion that the book would more than compensate for the fact that he was denied the opportunity to wear the crown. Unless Nkrumah unconsciously deceived himself as he so often did, nobody knew better than him that even placing a library of his books in every household was not bound to change much.

Chapter Twenty

On 13th May 1972, at the elaborate state funeral held for Nkrumah in Conakry, Guinea, Amilcar Cabral, the charismatic leader of Guinea Bissau, seemed to sum Nkrumah's tragedy all up when he said in his powerful tribute to Nkrumah:

"Nobody can tell us that Nkrumah died of a cancer of the throat or some other illness. No, Nkrumah was killed by the cancer of betrayal which we must uproot from Africa if we really want to bring about the final liquidation of imperialist domination from this continent…. As an African adage says, 'those who dare to spit at the sky only dirty their own faces'… We, the liberation movements, will not forgive those who betrayed Nkrumah. The people of Ghana will not forgive. Africa will not forgive. Progressive mankind will not forgive. Let those who still have to rehabilitate themselves in the eyes of Africa make haste to do so. It is not yet too late."

There could never have been a better epitaph for this great Ghanaian than this.

Incidentally, as part of the intrigue of betrayals, Cabral himself became a victim of a more sinister "cancer of betrayal" when he was assassinated in Conakry in January 1973, less than a year after his powerful speech. In Nkrumah's exile years in Conakry, the "cancer of betrayal" metamorphosed into varied scenarios.

From Conakry, Nkrumah made very strenuous but fruitless efforts to regain power in Ghana. An even much more serious effort to unseat the NLC military junta also failed. The query has always been why he was unsuccessful? On the 17 April 1967, there occurred a counter-coup by Lieutenants S. Arthur and M. Yeboah, in which General Emmanuel K. Kotoka, the NLC chairman, and some military officers were killed. Although Nkrumah had no foreknowledge of the 17 April counter-coup, he knew that had it succeeded he would most certainly have returned to Ghana. But he should have known better – that the idea of ousting Nkrumah had not emanated from any Ghanaian soldier, and that Kotoka and Afrifa and everyone else involved in the act had been used by the Western Intelligence. And so, any military attempt that had not received the blessings of the CIA, was bound to fail. The only sad thing about it, quite apart from the fact that it failed, was that General Kotoka, who had stacked up his own share of the booty in a Swiss Bank, never had the opportunity to sign it over to anybody else.

There were several other plots and counter-plots in Nkrumah's name, some of them faked, but as a result of varied levels of betrayals, none was successful. Sometimes some would-be coup plotters, conmen indeed, who had received money from Nkrumah for that purpose would go so far as to give a definite date when he could expect to hear the good news.

By far the severest blow came in the month of November, 1968. On the 16th of that November, at about midnight, there took place in Villa Syli, Nkrumah's residence, a meeting of Nkrumah's Political Committee along with CPP sympathisers and tin tanks from Europe and Africa, including Ghana. There was only one item on the agenda - Nkrumah's return to power in Ghana. It is true that no previous attempts to unseat the junta in Accra had succeeded. But that was mainly because the actions had never been seriously coordinated and financed. It was time for such a move to be given definitive form.

In attendance were President Sekou Touré, his host and the Malian Ambassador in Accra. From London were two very important personalities - Douglas Rogers, editor of the Nkrumah-government owned *Africa and the World* monthly magazine which published very sophisticated analyses of the Ghanaian situation, interspersed with editorials for the overthrow of the NLC regime, and, Ekow Eshun that very loyal London-based head of overseas wing of Nkrumah's CPP, coordinator of Pro-Nkrumah activities from London to West African capitals. There was also Dr. A. B. Assensoh, journalist; junior brother to Anthony Nelson Assensoh, once district commissioner in Nkrumah's government who now worked in league with R.O. Amoako-Atta, the Ashanti Regional commissioner to assist Dr. Assensoh in his activities to help the overthrow of the NLC; there was Nkrumah's Chief Protocol officer, Camara Sana and six other members of his personal security and intelligence in Conakry - Moses E. Appoh (Special Intelligence Officer and Deputy Chairman of Administrative Committee), Mathew Ackah Mensah (Head of Special Intelligence Unit and member of Administrative Committee), Ambrose Yankey Snr (Personal Assistant to the President), Ambrose Yankey Jnr (Special Intelligence Officer), Nyamikeh Nganyah (Personal Attendant to President and nephew of President), David Gharty (Special Intelligence Officer). And finally, though from the lower ranks, there was Amoah (Nkrumah's cook, an ex-army cook who had been in charge of his food long before the coup, and who had accompanied him to Hanoi) and W. Sarfo (Nkrumah's most trusted secretary).

There was also a certain retired Captain Kojo Tsikata whom Nkrumah had been persuaded to be part of the meeting. He had arrived Conakry with plans for a counter-coup. He was interviewed by Ambrose Yankey and two other members of the entourage. Nkrumah adamantly refused to see him. He believed that Tsikata had been implicated in an anti-CPP coup plot before 1966 and he did not trust him. Neither did the Guinean authorities.

The event opened with a short film about the American bombing and the rapid repair of damage to road and bridges, scenes illustrating the indomitable spirit of the Vietnamese people, totally committed to achieving victory. At the end of the film there was a clip in which a Vietnamese diplomat presented Nkrumah with rings made from the metal of destroyed US aircraft. Each ring was stamped with a number denoting the total number of American aircraft shot down at the time the ring was made.

In the keynote address which he himself delivered, with two of the rings on his forefinger and index finger, Kwame Nkrumah revoked his earlier pleas to the Ghanaian people to pray and eschew violent action. "Only the deliberately blind can fail to see that non-violence will lead us nowhere. Osageyefo can no longer sit back and watch his efforts, twenty years of relentless toil go down the drain.

"I hate to go back on my word," Nkrumah said. "But it is wishful thinking to sit back and hope that some miracle will overthrow the "Notorious Liars Commission whose every act seems designed to turn back the clock, through the deliberate dismemberment of our beloved country. They first removed me, the head, and now they are hell-bent on cutting off the arms and legs of Ghana, so that the star of Africa which had reached the sprinting level in its development, should go back to creeping. With what pleasure the neo-colonial imperialists would be watching! The Seven-Year Development Plan has been abandoned. And why not? The members of this petty-minded and treacherous clique of army and police which has had the effrontery to claim that they have taken over the government of Ghana, is too ignorant to realise that a planted seed takes time to germinate before sprouting into the glorious foliage that is visible to all.

"In their endless efforts to discredit the CPP they have nullified every positive achievement. For them to really justify the fact that the CPP had done nothing good for

138

Ghana they should have brought in caterpillars to uproot the bridges, tear down the Tema and Takoradi harbours, pulled down the Volta dam. They should have brought in their own experts to reintroduce an educational system that negates the free education which the CPP had instituted, and shut down the electrification network that that we set up, closed all the clinics, hospitals, health centres which are dotted all over the country. It is not enough to make a song of the false accusations that the CPP did more harm to Ghana than good. It is important to show this in concrete terms."

He made a casual reference to the Bismarckian philosophy of "Blood and Iron" when he said: "To bring Ghana out of the present morass will not be done through economic blockade and speeches from Conakry and elsewhere on constitutional change, but by blood and iron. Between March and December 1966 I addressed the Ghanaian people fifteen times from Conakry. I have written enough books to fill a library and each of which I have exhausted all my art of persuasion. But all that, as the saying goes, has been like pouring water on the duck's back.

"I will let the cat out of the bag in revealing that the failure encountered by my pan-African brother and comrade in arms, President Sekou Touré has taught us a valued lesson and has now made it necessary for us to put all our eggs in one basket, as it were. Three months ago he raised a force of the Guinean army to invade Ghana via Ivory Coast. President Houphuoet Boigny, that high priest of neo-colonialist stooges, declared that no soldier on his way to Ghana will set foot on his soil. And that was our only route. We have now decided to circumvent that obstacle by isolating him in this new operation which we have code named *FP – Final Push*. The aim of that operation is to bring all the militant heads of state of the OAU together – eleven in number - to raise a force and storm Ghana by sea, air and land through Lome. The necessary finances were being provided by China, and several other unnamed organisations. A new date has been set and a new point of convergence has been agreed upon. All our militant OAU member states are in the know and are waiting only for the order from us to charge. However, because of the dangers of our communication lines being tapped, we shall send our trusted agents to personally visit these capitals and make personal contacts. Our agents have long been infiltrating into Ghana, and linking up with CPP members on the spot to work together to overthrow the NLC at the appropriate moment. Our hotel in Accra which our men on the ground have code named **The Date**, is near completion. Two of our agents will leave this night immediately we disperse, with good money for getting everything ready, through the diplomatic bag of the Malian embassy at Accra…"

"Why do you give the hotel such a name?" somebody asked.

Since his arrival in Conakry Nkrumah had decided to be permanently dressed in white, which in Guinea was the dress that was worn during a mourning period. Nkrumah who was mourning for Ghana was wearing a white "political suit," a pair of trousers over which was worn a shirt that reached almost to the knees, which does not require a shirt and tie under and is buttoned right up to the neck. When the question was asked, he straightened the edges of the bottom of the shirt, smiled his knowing smile before saying in a low voice: "that refers to the date that Osagyefo will regain his rightful place in Ghana and in history."

"Boye Moses, that very senior member of our entourage involved in the planning of the "Operation Positive Action" is to lead a special intelligence mission. He will start travelling under a false name tomorrow, through Sierra Leone, Togo, Dahomey and Nigeria. Within three days it is hoped that he should be able to link up with other supporters on the ground, who are already expecting him. The Guinean government is already providing passports and other facilities, and has allowed its embassies to be used for the transmission of messages and weapons. I have been informed to move to Bamako by the 23rd November, considering its proximity to Upper Volta and the common frontier with Northern Ghana, just in case I may need to enter through the north."

Everything was put in place and it was agreed that on the night of the 26 November, the Guinean government and the entire Political Committee which was so convinced of the machinery they had put in place for invasion of Ghana was to invite Nkrumah to spend the night at Sekou Touré's residence so that he would be ready to make a broadcast as soon as the good news was reported. They would spend the night listening to the World Service of the BBC which they hoped would be glad to be one of the first teams on the sport during the second coming.

So sure was he of the plans that they began to work out how they would live on their return. When asked by Sekou Touré Nkrumah told them that he would not live in Flagstaff House or the Castle.

"You remember how I told you about Mao Tse Tung's "cave"?"

"Yeah, I remember," Sekou Touré responded.

"I will live largely in such an underground headquarter in the hills around Aburi, on the lines of the 'cave' of Chairman Mao in China. I would devote my time to organising the total liberation and unification of Africa, leaving the day to day administration of Ghana to the Party."

Nkrumah sketched a plan of his intended Aburi headquarters which he showed Sekou Touré and members of the Political Committee which they all approved of. He also read to them drafts of a broadcast (under the heading "The Task Ahead") concerning the announcement of emergency measures, and the long-term changes to be made on the 27th of May, the day after his arrival back in Ghana.

141

On its part, the NLC had no illusions about Nkrumah's ability to move people. They all knew him as an effective spell-binder and rabble rouser who could very effortlessly make his audience become incensed or sorrowful according to the effect he wished to produce. Therefore, they concluded that once Nkrumah was alive and in exile in nearby Guinea, the military government could not be as safe as they wanted. The most logical thing was to infiltrate Nkrumah's inner circle of former cabinet members.

Two days after the Political Committee meeting in Conakry, **the Special Executive for Counter Espionage** also met in an emergency session in Accra. This was made up of the NLC Intelligence Unit, Ghana's Special Branch of the internal security unit attached to the Ghana Police Service and Ghana Foreign Service officers from the Research Bureau (the Foreign Ministry's intelligence unit). The NLC intelligence was so good that minutes of the meeting of the Nkrumah Political Committee meeting were reported to the NLC verbatim. No weapon in the arsenal of sabotage was too mean for them to employ, from blackmail to outright murder or elimination. For example, they used blackmail to win Nkrumah's CPP supporters and ex-ministers to their side. Towards that end, the financial records of ex-CPP men and women were examined. It showed that most of them lived in government-owned bungalows at Kanda Estate in Accra.

Even as those CPP stalwarts were thrown into jail, their wives and families continued to live in the houses. The NLC threatened to evict them. To save their families, many of them turned traitors. These CPP leaders on whom Nkrumah counted for a return to power, became turncoats and assisted the NLC to thwart Nkrumah's efforts. That was even how the NLC came to know that there was a hotel being built to house Nkrumah's supporters and that preparations in the form of agents travelling across the entire West Africa were afoot for Nkrumah's return.

Consequently, all the Pro-Nkrumah activities were frustrated. It comprised spies posted to embassies in West Africa to monitor the activities of Nkrumah and his numerous agents, as well as the pro-NLC diplomatic mission set up in Conakry as an intelligence post to monitor Nkrumah's agents coming in and out of Guinea. The emergency **Special Executive for Counter Espionage** meeting which was attended by senior members of the NLC, was chaired by Dr. Hilla Hilmann – a top Research Bureau employee at the time, serving as a head of the chancellery at the Ghana embassy in Lome, Togo, with responsibility for intelligence and to checkmate pro-Nkrumah activities in Togo. Educated at the London School of Economics and La Sorbonne in Paris he once boasted to some arrested ex-CPP members from Conakry that "Even when Nkrumah coughs in Guinea, we know it." He would prove that that was no overstatement. For, while the Nkrumah camp was preparing and expecting news and preparing too for his triumphant return to Ghana, the counter intelligence force of the NLC backed by its Western allies, began to score major points which were sure to send Nkrumah to an early grave.

First, in the morning of 19 November 1968, three days after the Political Committee meeting in Conakry, the Malian government of President Modibo Keita was overthrown in a *coup d'état*, which the pro-Nkrumah camp said must have been sponsored by the CIA and or its Western allies. The NLC was sufficiently informed of the important role Mali was given to play in the comeback venture. So, the very next day, thanks to the intensified Research Bureau activities, the NLC sent General Afrifa to Mali to warn the new military junta there about its embassy's pro-Nkrumah activities in Accra. At the same time, several pro-Nkrumah agents were rounded up and either "neutralised" or murdered inside Ghana. The public was informed of the dangers involved in any persons attempting to put foot in the vicinity of the hotel.

And there was more bad news: on the 25th of November news came to the Political Committee that all their emissaries had been captured. Arriving Dahomey on the 23 November, Boye Moses had fallen into the NLC dragnet. He had been immediately flown to Ghana where he was paraded on national TV and through the streets of Accra in a cage. Also, he entered Cotonou on his spy mission and to acquaint their supporters in the other West African capitals Ekow Eshun was picked up. Information from CPP traitors in Conakry had been relayed to CPP leaders in Ghana who were working as double agents for the NLC. He was immediately taken to Ghana and humiliated publicly to serve as a lesson to other Nkrumah agents. He too appeared on TV virtually naked, his hands tied behind him and being pulled this way and that way, to the amusement of the NLC onlookers.

On 27 November 1968, the day Nkrumah was supposed to have been addressing the Ghanaians from Accra, they found themselves worse off than ever before. At the behest of Ambrose Yankey, a soul-searching meeting was summoned that evening. The main issue at stake was the continuous betrayals even from within the team in Conakry. Nkrumah was so despondent that he declined to say anything, although he was present. There was only one item on the agenda: who were the traitors amongst them?

"Surely, the NLC is not made of magicians," Ambrose Yankey said. "Most of us sitting in here right now, are not CPP at heart. Or if they are CPP, they are also many things else. Many of us in here now know that they are double agents who have been bought over by the NLC with which they are in direct and minute by minute touch. Otherwise how can we explain the fact that within a few hours after our secret meeting here, the NLC had received all the details of the movements of our agents? Let us be honest to expose these individuals here and now, if we are not to forget about returning to Ghana."

144

Nkrumah was right that there were traitors amongst them. The first person to speak was Amoah, his cook. The faithful cook shocked everybody when he revealed that in the evening of the day of the Political Committee meeting Captain Tsikata came up to him and offered him a bribe of $1000 for him to poison Osagyefo. (For this revelation, Amoah died a week later. It was given that he had died of cancer of the liver. Although the Nkrumaists suspected real foul play, they were loath to give the NLC credit for their expert intelligence work by infiltrating their own security network so successfully as to poison Nkrumah's cook).

Although Captain Tsikata tried unconvincingly to swear his innocence, he also implicated one other person: Wellington Sarfo – Nkrumah's most trusted secretary. This accusation was supported partly by the fact that Sarfo made no attempt to defend himself and partly by Camara Sana. According to Sana:

"Sarfo was really in a position to leak sensitive information because he is responsible for typing letters, messages and cables. Furthermore, his desk is on the veranda of the villa in a position from where he can see every visitor, and often hear conversations."

In the midst of all these treacheries, the Portuguese ships attacked on 22 November 1970 with the aim of seizing Sekou Touré, Nkrumah and Amilcar Cabral. In an early morning assault, and relying on information from Guinea-based informants, the Portuguese attacks were directed at the Belle Vue (but Nkrumah was no longer living there) as well as the official presidential residence in Conakry, and another one housing Cabral. Guinean forces repulsed the attacks and several mercenaries were captured, including their alleged leader, one Captain Fernando.

Each of these, a monumental setback of unprecedented proportion, drilled a nail into Nkrumah's coffin and pushed him more and more into his grave. These failures in themselves constituted as much poison as one can possibly imagine.

And again, all this happening to a man who once saw himself as too big for Ghana alone to own. So big, that Ghana ought to share him with the rest of Africa. And now, having risen from prisoner to President, his life seemed to have gone full circle. For, in Guinea, even though he was virtually under house arrest, he was guarded like a convicted felon, his empire now shrunk to just a few metres. Students of literature will recall William Shakespeare's Mark Antony's lamentation over the dead Caesar:

O mighty Caesar! Dost thou lie so low?
Are all thy conquests, glories, triumphs, spoils,
Shrunk to this little measure? Fare thee well.

How appropriate! When Amilcar Cabral underscored the "cancer of betrayal" that killed Nkrumah in 1972, therefore, it was neither a gainsaying nor an exaggeration. His words, indeed, shook many anti-Nkrumah elements as well as his treacherous political associates and fortune hunters who undermined his plans to regain power.

Epilogue

Whatever the reasons advanced either by the coup plotters or by their paymasters, the coup of 24 February 1966 had only one goal – the removal of Kwame Nkrumah from power, whose presence was too irksome to the neo-colonial masters. It was not to help Ghana in any way. Of course, the relatives of those who had been imprisoned for one reason or the other rejoiced at the overthrow. Furthermore, friends and relatives of the coup plotters became instantly rich from the booty that the traitors got. But there the benefits of the coup ended. It did not usher in the predicted millennium. To the total satisfaction of the Western powers, Ghana became the laughingstock of the world overnight, and had to carry its begging bowl from one economic capital of the West to the other. As could have been expected, nothing happened of significant note outside the spasmodic and frantic efforts by the NLC to prevent Nkrumah from coming back.

We said the coup did not achieve anything, but, in an ironic sense, it achieved very much: it threw open the floodgates of disorder. Kotoka fell under the bullets of the abortive coup of 1967; Ankrah who took over as Chairman of the NLC, was disgraced and forced to resign in 1969 over a corruption scandal; Brigadier Afrifa who succeeded him was only too happy to return the country to civilian rule so as to retire and enjoy the wealth his involvement in the coup had brought him. Dr. Kofi Busia, Nkrumah's arch antagonist who won the elections of 1969, ruled for only a year before he was overthrown by Colonel Acheampong; in 1967 a palace coup led by General Akouffo overthrew Acheampong.

The rigmarole continued unabated as Akuoffo himself was executed along with eight former leaders including General Afrifa, by Flight Lt. Jerry Rawlings in 1979; he returned the country once again to civilian rule with Hilla Hilmann as the new Head of State, but a few years later Rawlings returned. It was only with Rawlings' second coming that a semblance of stability set in.

The End